Kate Walden Directs

Kate Walden Directs:
NIGHT OF THE
ZOMBIE
CHICKENS

Julie Mata

DISNEY • HYPERION

LOS ANGELES • NEW YORK

First Hardcover Edition, May 2014
First Paperback Edition, April 2015
1 3 5 7 9 10 8 6 4 2
J689-1817-1-15032
Designed by Marci Senders
ISBN 978-1-4847-1664-9

Library of Congress Control Number for Hardcover Edition: 2014001110

Visit www.DisneyBooks.com

SUSTAINABLE FORESTRY INITIATIVE

Certified Chain of Custody
Promoting Sustainable Forestry

www.sfiprogram.org
SFI-01054

The SFI label applies to the text stock

To Antonio,
who always believed in this story,
who never said no, not even to chickens.
Con todo mi amor.

• • •

And for my mother, who taught me how to write,
and my father, who taught me what is right.

The last normal day of my life is a Saturday, and it starts pretty much like every other morning. When I go downstairs to the kitchen, my dad rattles his newspaper and my mother mumbles something in my direction and yawns. They both still have zombie faces, so I know they haven't drunk enough coffee yet. Wilma, our terrier, jumps all over me, whining and crying like she hasn't seen me in a year.

My mother's cooking eggs and the whole kitchen reeks, so I hold my nose as I eat a bowl of cereal. I hate everything about eggs. They're like nature's practical joke. They break if you barely touch them, and their disgusting glop oozes everywhere. Once they're cooked, they taste like boiled jellyfish. Worst of all, eggs come from chickens. Don't even get me started on chickens.

I can feel my mother studying me as I hold my nose, like she's wondering if it's a battle worth fighting. Finally she just sighs and cracks another egg into the pan.

My dad pours himself a coffee refill, then looks over his newspaper at me. The caffeine is finally kicking in. "So, Kate, what's the plan for today?"

"Alyssa's coming over."

"What are you two doing?"

"Working on my movie."

"You need any more zombies?" He makes his best evil zombie face.

"You've already been a zombie," I remind him. "And you got killed off, so it would be weird if you showed up again."

He butters his toast and thinks about it. "I could wear a disguise, like a beard and a Panama hat. Or it could be like *Night of the Living Dead*—you know, zombies that come back from the grave, over and over."

My dad is a big fan of the movie I'm making. My mother isn't so sure. She tries to hide it, but I can tell.

I've made tons of short movies with friends, but when I came up with the idea for *Night of the Zombie Chickens*, I knew it had to be a real movie. Feature-length. Anyway, I read on a moviemaking Web site that if you want to be a director, the best way to learn is to just do it. Just make a movie. So that's what I'm doing. And they're right. I've learned plenty, mostly the hard way.

Night of the Zombie Chickens is about a girl named

Mallory who lives on a farm and hates eggs. She refuses to eat them, which is lucky for her. Very lucky.

From the corner of my eye, I see my mother toss down half a cup of coffee in one gulp and wipe her mouth.

"Have you fed the hens, Kate?" she asks, suddenly all business. Definitely payback for holding my nose.

I pour myself another bowl of cereal. Anything to put off the terrible moment. "Why do I always have to feed them? Why can't Derek ever do it?"

"We've already been through this. You feed the chickens, and Derek takes out the garbage and mows the lawn."

"But I have tons of work to do for my shoot today." I look to my dad, but he stays safely behind his newspaper. "I have to get all the props together, and I have to figure out the lighting, and I need more blood. . . ."

"Chores come first." There's an edge to my mother's voice. I know I'm on thin ice. Whining first thing in the morning is a risky move in our house.

"I bet George Lucas doesn't have to do chores before he makes a movie," I mutter.

My mother decides to try a different tactic. "You don't want your leading ladies to starve, do you?"

My mother thinks I should feel responsible for the hens since they have roles in my movie. Personally I think the ladies could stand to lose a few pounds. Sometimes directors hit it off great with their movie stars, but other times they end up hating each other. I'd say the hens and I have a love-hate relationship. I love deep-fried chicken and they hate me.

You'd think they would be thrilled to do something exciting for once in their lives, instead of pecking at bugs and squirting out eggs day after day. But working with chickens has been worse than a zombie's nightmare. They can't cackle on cue or hit their marks or deliver a single crazed stare at the camera when I need it. Mostly they just run away and scratch at the grass.

At first, I thought maybe they were just too dumb. After all, chickens will poop in their own food if you let them, which is pretty revolting. But then I started to wonder. I got chills down my spine when I watched the movie *Chicken Run*, because some days, just like Mr. Tweedy, I could swear those hens are up to something.

Paranoid? Maybe—but consider this. It sounds like something right out of a movie, but it happened to me. It was just a normal day, except I was in a hurry, so I wore my flip-flops into the chicken coop instead of my mom's old boots. A hen decided my toes were worms and wanted to make them into a meal. When I kicked her away, my flip-flop flew off and hit her right in the head. It was an accident, but it was kind of funny, so I laughed.

I don't think hens like to be laughed at.

I refilled the feeders, then hurried to the door. It happened so fast I never saw it coming. A hen ran under my feet, and I tripped and fell right into a fresh, steaming mound of chicken poop. There I was, flat out on the chicken coop floor, dazed, smeared with greenish crap, and up waddled the hen that tried to eat my toes. She stood there, clucking, and then...

She *winked* at me.

Now, my mother can argue all she wants that it wasn't the same hen, or that the poop wasn't strategically placed, or that hens can't wink, but I know what I saw. So I don't trust hens and I don't like visiting the coop. If it were up to me, those ladies would all go on a diet, starting today.

2

There should be a law that parents aren't allowed to make their kids work on Saturdays. It's the absolute best day of the week, and nothing ruins it faster than chores. And no chore is worse than feeding chickens, except maybe cleaning out their coop. I stir my cereal, trying to think of a way to get out of my job. Nothing comes to mind. "They're your chickens," I finally mutter. "Why do I have to feed them? They're disgusting."

Sure enough, my mother slaps the spatula down on the stove, and I know I've gone too far. Derek can call me warthog and she'll just shake her head, but talk trash about her hens and her feathers really get ruffled.

"You are a member of this family, and you have responsibilities," she lectures. "In the old days, children on a farm spent hours doing chores before they even had breakfast. You and Derek have it easy."

My mother watched way too many episodes of *Little House on the Prairie* when she was young. You'd think she had to feed the pigs and milk the cows and slog through five miles of snow to school every day. The truth is, she grew up in a suburb near Detroit and rode a school bus. Anyway, we don't live on a farm, just a tiny five-acre farmette.

I also know better than to point any of this out. I stuff my mouth with a doughnut just to make sure I don't let loose with a snappy comeback. That's a sure ticket to getting stuck cleaning out the chicken coop.

Derek trudges in with a nasty case of bed head. His eyes are crusted over and his mouth hangs open like an overstretched rubber band. He collapses in a seat and drops his head in his arms. As soon as my mother slaps a plate of eggs in front of him, though, he perks up and digs right in. That kid will eat anything. He sticks his fork into the yolks, and I have to cover my eyes so I don't see the yellow goo spurting out like alien eyeball juice.

Everyone else in my family loves eggs, which is a good thing, since that's my mother's new business—raising organic chickens and selling their meat and eggs. She used to dress in suits and heels every day and look really sharp. Right now, she's in baggy work pants and big shin-kicking boots, with an old bandanna tied around her head. She looks like a farmhand, but she says it's the best thing that ever happened to her, except for getting married and having Derek and me.

My dad folds his newspaper and looks at me. "Well, if you decide you need an extra scary guy, let me know."

"I don't need a zombie," I tell him. "But maybe you could be my gaffer."

"Ha-ha," Derek pipes up. "Dad's going to be a gasser—he's good at that." Derek never misses a chance to joke about gas and farting. Luckily he's only in fifth grade, so we go to different schools. I'm in seventh grade at Medford Junior High. I already feel sorry for the teachers there, knowing Derek and his friends will descend on them next year.

I roll my eyes at Derek. "Gaffer. It's the guy in charge of lighting. The scene takes place in the basement, but it's too dark down there. We need to add some light."

"Lighting, check. I can do that," my dad says.

The guys who make movies practically have their own language. I'm keeping my own cheat sheet on all the lingo. Mostly I pick it up from Web sites on moviemaking. For instance, a plain old clothespin is called a C-47. I guess saying "Toss me that clothespin" doesn't sound fancy enough on a big Hollywood set.

"Isn't it time to wrap up this movie?" my mother asks in an overly cheery voice. "I bet you have lots of other ideas for movies."

She knows this is a sensitive subject. I've been trying to come up with an ending for *Night of the Zombie Chickens* for months. I polish off the rest of my cereal and slurp up the milk.

"You can't rush art," I tell her. She probably wants me to make a gushy romance.

"That's right," my dad adds. "We could have a budding Spielberg here. We don't want to spoil her vision." He gives my mother a look to remind her that she needs to nurture my delicate preteen self-esteem.

My mother sighs as she scrubs out the frying pan. "All I'm saying is that most movies are only an hour and a half long."

Everybody's a critic. Sure, *Night of the Zombie Chickens* is probably three hours long by now, but it takes time to build a story.

My main character, Mallory, the girl who hates eggs, finds out that the local chicken feed company has been putting ground-up human bones in their product to save money. The problem is, the bones came from a graveyard that was a secret dumping ground for toxic chemicals, so all the local hens have been snacking on a foul stew of rotted bones and polluted muck.

The first time she read my script, my mother squinted like the light hurt her eyes. "Why chicken feed?" she asked.

I shrugged. "We have chickens. I need actors."

"I'm trying to run a business here, Kate. My hens are not toys for you to play with."

"I'm not playing," I protested. "Making movies is a business, too."

My mother shook her head. "There is no way that—"

Then my dad put an arm around her shoulder. He gave her another one of his looks. "Now, Jean, I don't think it would hurt the hens to unleash a little of their inner DiCaprio."

My dad has been super supportive of this whole crazy organic hen operation from the start. He agreed to move to the farmette and he was okay with my mom quitting her job, even though it means we have a lot less money to live on. I know, because sometimes I hear them arguing about money late at night when they think Derek and I are asleep. I asked my dad about it once, and he said they weren't arguing—they were just *discussing*—but it was a pretty loud discussion.

Since the move, my dad has spent most of his weekends fixing problems with the house and building chicken pens. So after she got "the look," my mother sighed and told me her company, Heavenly Hens, should get a special mention in the movie credits.

Anyway, it's not the length of my movie that bothers my mom. It's the plot. After the hens eat the bad feed, they start acting weird. At first no one notices. By the time people realize the hens have turned into berserk zombies, it's too late. Mallory's entire family, her neighbors, and, in fact, the whole town have all eaten the polluted eggs. Everyone turns into zombies and goes running around the countryside trying to turn Mallory into a zombie, too.

Still, as much as I hate to admit it, my mother is right. I need to come up with an ending. It's starting to keep me awake at night. I lie in bed and gnaw on my fingernails, puzzling over the last scene. Should it be tragic? Romantic? Explosive? Nothing seems right.

"So give us a hint," my dad says. "Does Mallory turn into a zombie herself? Does she escape and find true love?"

I stare at my empty cereal bowl, but no flash of genius hits me. "I don't know. I can't decide how it should end."

The missing last scene feels like a weight pressing down on my gut. Or maybe I just ate too much. I'm so full I can't swallow another bite, which means the worst part of my day has arrived. I push my chair back from the table with a loud protest screech and trudge outside.

It's a sunny blue-sky day. The air is so crisp and clean I wish I were shooting. Hollywood movies spend a lot of money trying to create this shimmery morning glow. On days like this, I don't mind living out in the country so much. Until I step into the chicken coop. As soon as I open the door, three hens try to dart past me. I manage to shoo two back inside, but one escapes.

The hens get to roam around outdoors, but not until the afternoon. In the mornings, they have to stay in the coop until they've laid their eggs. That means I have to catch the hen. But I can hardly run because my stomach is so full. I hurry after her, but she flaps her wings and darts away.

"I hate eggs!" I say loudly, to see if I get a reaction. She pecks at the grass, pretending to ignore me, but every time I move closer, she scurries away. "Chickens are dumb as rocks," I call after her. I laugh out loud just to show I'm still in control.

The hen cocks her head and blinks her beady eyes at me. Finally I get an idea. I grab a handful of grass and sing out, "Chick chick chick," which is how I call them at feeding time. I throw the grass into the air like it's feed, and sure enough the hen darts forward. See what I mean about dumb?

I return her to the coop, then refill the feeders and the waterers. I grab a basket and collect the eggs that have been laid so far this morning. As I turn to go, I notice an egg lying in a corner of the coop. This is strange because the hens almost always lay their eggs in the laying boxes. The egg is funny-shaped, more like a potato. It turns out the shell is paper-thin. As soon as I pick it up, it cracks open and the most ghastly, horrendous, unspeakable odor fills the coop. The air turns green, or maybe it's just my eyes going blind from the rotten fumes.

I stumble toward the door, my stomach churning from the horror of it all. I don't make it. Instead, I puke up my entire breakfast right there in the coop. Which the hens start to eat. Did I mention that chickens are revolting? I wipe my mouth and stagger outside into the fresh air. As the door slams shut behind me, I swear I hear the sound of chicken laughter.

When I tell my mother what happened, she totally dismisses the idea that the rotten egg was a revenge plot. "You've been watching too many movies," she scolds. And then she starts worrying—not about her daughter, who just lost her entire breakfast—but about her hens. My favorite cereal is green and pink and blue, and it's definitely not organic. So my mother starts squawking that I shouldn't have left my breakfast behind for the hens to snack on. She runs outside and never even asks me how I feel.

My dad puts an arm around my shoulder and squeezes. I know he's probably thinking the same thing I am—that my mother prefers a bunch of organic, free-range, overachieving, diabolical hens to me.

3

Alyssa Jensen plays the part of Mallory in *Night of the Zombie Chickens*. She's been my BFF since first grade. She wants to be a Hollywood actress, so she really knows how to scream and get worked up. Alyssa has long legs and long arms and long blond hair. She totally looks like an actress, except sometimes her face breaks out. On a bad day, she obsesses about it in front of the mirror and squirts weird ointments on her face while I tell her she looks fine. Luckily, when she comes over later Saturday morning, her skin looks clear.

She brushes her hair in front of my mirror as we lounge in my room. Alyssa has always been taller than me, so sometimes people think she's older. She's only in seventh grade, but recently two different strangers asked her if she was in high school. It doesn't bother me. Well, maybe a little. No one ever thinks I'm in high school. Just last week the supermarket cashier asked if I was in a sixth-grade class with her daughter. I tell myself it's just because I'm short. Still, I shoot a sideways look at Alyssa in the mirror and sigh.

"Who's the zombie of the week?" she asks.

That's a standing joke because I've had so many people play zombies by now that I've pretty much run out of actors. One Saturday afternoon we even threw a picnic and invited all the neighbors. When we were done eating, they put on their zombie clothes and chased Alyssa around the yard. It's one of my favorite scenes.

I hesitate because I know Alyssa won't like the answer. "Derek," I finally say. "And his friend Trevor."

Alyssa groans. "I thought you said he wasn't allowed in your movie."

"They're the only ones left. The mailman said no."

"Maybe it's time to finish this movie, Hitch. I mean, seriously, how many more ways can a zombie attack me?"

Hitch is her nickname for me, after Alfred Hitchcock, one of my favorite directors. I had a bizarre nightmare about bloodthirsty attack hens after I saw his creepy movie *The Birds*. That's what gave me the idea for *Night of the Zombie Chickens*.

Alyssa fidgets with a bottle on my dresser. "I mean, aren't you kind of tired of working on this? It takes up so much time."

I'm so surprised that my mouth actually drops open. Alyssa and I have been making movies together for years. It's the first time she's ever sounded *tired* of it.

"It's almost done," I say slowly. "I'm working on the last scene." Which is true, if you count the hours I've spent thinking about it. "Anyway, it's good practice for you. It's not easy to become a Hollywood actress."

Alyssa shrugs. "Yeah, I guess."

But her voice sounds bored. Alyssa must notice my face because she quickly says, "I want to finish it! I'm just saying, maybe next time we should try a romance. Something where I get to wear a dress and I don't have to scream. I read somewhere that if you overwork your voice when you're young, you can get lesions on your throat."

Now she's starting to sound like my mother. What's gotten into her? "A romance? Are you joking? Who would play the lead?"

"Scot Logan," she says with a grin. I snort because Scot Logan only comes up to her chin.

"Nathaniel Morgan," I offer. She throws me a nasty look. Nathaniel is a squinty, skinny boy who's liked her since fifth grade. "Or how about . . . Jake Knowles?" I say slyly.

Alyssa has had a crush on Jake Knowles for three years. That's a long time in girl years. She keeps insisting she's way over him, but I'm not convinced.

She gives a dismissive snort. "Yuck." But a second later,

she gazes dreamily at herself in the mirror like she's trying to imagine how Jake might do as a romantic lead.

"They're all yuck," I say. "I'd rather have a zombie chasing me any day."

"Fine. But you seriously need to come up with an ending."

"I'm trying! But you're the only normal person left, remember? I want to have a happy ending, but it's kind of hard when everyone else is trying to turn you into a zombie."

We look at each other and then we both crack up. To a stranger, our conversations would sound pretty strange.

"Remember that old couple at Mickey D's?" Alyssa asks.

I was just about to open my mouth to remind *her* about them. That's the great thing about Alyssa—we've known each other so long we pretty much have the exact same memories.

I nod happily. "Yeah, I thought they were going to call the police."

"Remember the old guy's face when we were talking about the best way to run someone over with a riding mower?"

"Yeah, and what about his wife? I thought she was going to lose her french fries when I said we needed a bigger blood splatter."

We're both laughing by now. We've probably had this exact same conversation half a dozen times already, but it doesn't matter. In fact, it only makes it better. It's like eating your favorite food—the longer you've been eating it, the better it gets.

I guess I can't blame Alyssa for getting tired of *Night of the Zombie Chickens*. We have been working on it a long time. Even your favorite food will get old if you eat it *too* often. I need to come up with an ending, quick.

Anyone who thinks it's easy to write and direct a movie is crazy. It's a lot of work, especially when there's zero budget and no crew. Still, I already know that making movies is what I want to do. Why? Because most of the time, real life is about as exciting as melting Jell-O. I love how Hollywood can make changing your socks look like high drama. In movies, animals can talk, people can fly, and chickens can turn into zombies. *Anything* can happen (if your budget is big enough). I can take my wildest dream and make it real. That's why I want to make movies. That's why, one day, I will be a big-time, big-budget Hollywood director.

4

Alyssa has gone back to brushing her hair. It looked fine ten minutes ago, but I try to be patient. Secretly I've always been a little envious of Alyssa's hair. It's blond and shiny and straight. Mine is brown and frizzy. In fact, it's no big secret that Alyssa is prettier than I am. My mom says we're pretty in different ways, but that's because she's my mom, so she has to say that. My dad says I'm beautiful and Derek says I'm pug ugly, so I'm guessing I'm somewhere in between.

Alyssa finally sets down the brush. "Maybe I should build a raft and float away on a river like I'm finding a new life."

"There's no river near here," I remind her.

She looks over, suddenly excited. "Speaking of water, did you hear what happened to Lydia?"

"She drowned?" I ask in a bored voice.

Alyssa snickers. "Yeah, wouldn't that be nice? Jack Timner pushed her into the pool at the Y last night and her bathing suit top almost came off and Jack got kicked out."

"She probably untied it herself just to get some attention," I grumble. "Like she doesn't get enough already."

Lydia Merritt is the MPG of our class—most popular girl. I've seen girls actually push each other just to stand next to her so they could laugh at her jokes and soak up the glow of her popularity. Picture a pretty girl with a motor mouth, and everything she says is ten decibels above everyone else. Then picture her sailing down the hallway, flip-flops flapping, gum snapping, laughter screeching, surrounded by eager wannabes, and that gives you a pretty good idea of Lydia Merritt. She looks like she could be in high school, too, maybe because of all the makeup she wears.

Completely out of the blue, Alyssa says: "You know, Lydia's never been a zombie. Why don't you ask her?"

I'm shoving a cookie in my mouth, and I actually spew crumbs at this. After I hack and cough, I finally get enough oxygen to wheeze, "Are you nuts?" It occurs to me that maybe Alyssa's been chased by one too many zombies. Lydia would probably be polite on the phone if I were crazy enough to call her, but I'm not about to provide her with yet another *Pathetic Kid Tries to Be Lydia's Friend* story. She already has enough of those. Not that I'm pathetic. But I'd sound that way.

Alyssa fiddles with a lock of her hair. "I was telling everyone about your movie yesterday and how you want to be a director, and Lydia overheard me. She thought it was really cool, you know, that it's about zombies."

"Wait a minute." I sit up. "Where was this? And who is 'everybody'?"

"A bunch of people were just hanging out in the park last night."

She says it carelessly, but I feel a stab of jealousy. Before we moved to the farmette, I lived five blocks from Alyssa's house and right around the corner from Granger Park, the neighborhood hangout. I could run over to Alyssa's whenever I felt like it. Now every time I want to do something, it has to be scheduled. It's a half-hour ride into town, so I end up missing the get-togethers in the park and the last-minute trips to the YMCA to shoot hoops. I miss just about everything.

"What was Lydia doing there?" I ask. "I thought she lived on the other side of town."

"Her parents got divorced last summer, remember? Her mom got a place on Sycamore Street, so she and her sister live there now."

Sycamore Street is just a few blocks from my old house, which makes Alyssa and Lydia practically neighbors. I feel another twinge of jealousy.

Alyssa has grown quiet and I know why. She's thinking about her own parents. They divorced when she was only nine. I still remember crying with Alyssa the day she found out. Mr. and Mrs. Jensen were like my second parents. I couldn't understand why they wanted to split up. I still don't really get it. For a long time, Alyssa hoped they would get back together, but last year her dad remarried. She was so upset that she almost didn't go to the wedding.

"I know Lydia's kind of annoying," Alyssa tells me, "but she was practically begging to be in your movie. So I told her she'd be a good zombie...." She breaks off when I glare at her. "I had to say something! She kept asking me questions. I told her you're always looking for zombies and maybe you'd call her." She says this last part in a rush.

And here's the thing—I make a huge *you traitor* face at Alyssa, but secretly I'm kind of pleased. Lydia Merritt thinks my movie sounds cool. Which it is. But still. I get a funny tingle at the idea of Lydia coming over to my house, chumming around with us. What is it about fame and its feeble cousin, popularity, that makes normal people turn into mindless zombies? Alyssa senses I'm not totally dismissing the idea.

"You have to admit, she'd be a lot better than Derriere and his weirdo friend." *Derriere*, which is French for *butt*, is her nickname for Derek. He calls her Duh-lyssa. They're definitely a mutual fan club. Alyssa hates that nickname, probably because her best subjects in school are gym and choir. After that, her grades go downhill fast. Derek only calls her that from a safe distance, because it definitely sends her off the deep end.

The upshot is, after endless discussion, decisions, reversals, nervous screams, and picking up the phone and banging it down a dozen times, I finally call Lydia's cell phone number, which, it turns out, she gave to Alyssa. I'm praying she won't answer, but Lydia picks up right away, like she's been waiting for me. As soon as I hear her voice, I wish I hadn't called. My face gets hot and my brain freezes over, but it's too late. Lydia's waiting and I have to say something.

"Uh, hi, Lydia, it's Kate Walden."

"Kate!" she screeches. "The zombie director! That is so cool you're making a movie! Alyssa told me about it, and I'm totally jealous she's the star. When do *I* get to be a zombie?"

That's Lydia. She can totally charm you in half a second. I try to remember why I don't like her. Even I have to admit, Lydia is pretty nice.

Deep breath. "That's why I'm calling. Alyssa and I are shooting another scene today and we need a zombie." My mind is whirling. Should I try to be funny? *I was going to use my little brother, so that just tells you how desperate we are, ha-ha.* But if it doesn't come off right, it will just sound lame. I decide to play it safe. "I was wondering if you might want to do it?"

A loud, ear-ringing screech. "Are you kidding? Should I wear zombie clothes? What *are* zombie clothes? I've got these ripped jeans, and I could mess up my hair—oh, and I've got a vial of fake blood from last Halloween, only I think it might be dried up, but I could bring it along, and I've got black nail polish, and I've got some vampire teeth. Do zombies have fangs?"

I have to admit, I've never had such an excited zombie, except maybe my dad. We get all the wardrobe stuff taken care of, and Lydia announces that her mom will Google our address and she'll be there in an hour. I get off the phone feeling nervous. Really nervous. Because a lot can go wrong. And because I've just invited the MPG of our class to my home . . . and my home happens to be a chicken farm.

Everyone I know lives within the city limits of Medford except me. We live in a farmhouse that was built a zillion years ago. It's been "updated" over the years, which means it looks like it's from the nineteen seventies instead of the eighteen seventies. It's got orange shag carpeting and fake wood paneling in the TV room. The bathtub is harvest gold, which is secret code for puke-colored. We moved here a year ago after my mom decided she really wanted to be an organic chicken farmer. She says we're going to redecorate as soon as we have the money, but now that she's quit her high-paying job, that could be a while.

The kitchen is the worst. It has a border near the ceiling with clownish roosters doing silly things: crowing, running—there's even a rooster *talking on an old-fashioned telephone*. I wince whenever I look at it, but my mom thinks it's cute.

Another thought stops me cold. What will Lydia think of the real chickens? They're free-range, which means my mother lets them wander all over our acreage. My dad is building a huge pen so they can roam outdoors and still be protected from foxes and hawks, but it isn't finished yet. Hopefully Lydia will think they're cute. I don't have time to worry about it, because I still need to whip up a batch of fake blood.

Making good fake blood is an art form, and I've become a bit of an expert. First, I have to decide how much blood I'll need. Sometimes all I need is a cup. For the riding mower scene, I made a gallon, and it took me an entire day to wash down the garage.

I love making blood. I feel a little like Dr. Frankenstein as I carefully measure out the ingredients. First, I dump some cornstarch and warm water into a bowl and stir them together. Once it's smooth, I add corn syrup and a few tablespoons of red food coloring. Finally, I reach for my secret ingredient.

The trick is to get the right color and texture. My early batches were too thick, and they ended up looking like watery cherry Jell-O. Definitely not scary.

My secret ingredient isn't really so secret, because I found the recipe on the Internet. It works really well, though. My blood was always the wrong color until I discovered powdered cocoa. Cocoa makes a deeper, darker red—something Count Dracula would really love to sink his fangs into.

I stir and fuss, adding a little more cocoa, until finally my blood is perfect. The first couple of times I made up a batch, Alyssa and I would dip our hands in the blood and pretend our fingers had been cut off, or we'd roll back our eyes and let it dribble out of our mouths. But now we don't even bother. We'd probably make great surgeons because the sight of buckets of blood doesn't bother us at all.

As I store the blood in a Tupperware container, a thought hits me. What if Lydia thinks my fake blood is stupid? I show the batch to Alyssa to see what she thinks. She swirls it around and holds it up to the light like it's a fine wine. She dips in a finger, inspects the red smear, then licks it off.

"Perfect," she announces. "Lydia will love this."

I grin at her. Alyssa's right—what's not to love about fake blood? Of course Lydia will think it's cool. She'll probably scream and want to dip her whole hand in it.

Still, some girls would get squeamish around fake blood, or they'd worry about staining their clothes. That's the great thing about Alyssa. She's always game for just about any crazy idea.

Once, when I still lived in town, I decided to climb Medford's old water tower after I saw Leonardo DiCaprio climb one in a movie. I thought about trying the new tower, but it was way too tall, and the security fence looked nasty.

The old tower was perfect, though, just waiting for some-one to climb it. Judging from the graffiti, a lot of people already had.

"You're nuts," Alyssa said when I told her. "I wouldn't climb that thing if you paid me a million dollars."

"It will be an adventure," I told her. "If we don't do crazy things now, pretty soon we'll be too old."

"Jumping backward off the high dive is crazy," she told me. "Climbing the water tower is suicidal."

"Leonardo did it in a movie," I pointed out, but Alyssa just rolled her eyes.

I set my alarm super early one Saturday morning and hopped on my bicycle. The sun was a round yellow yolk on the horizon as I pedaled to the edge of town. I imagined someone taking a huge fork and poking it until it broke. Would there be a nuclear explosion of gooey light pouring down Medford's streets? I filed the idea away for a possible future movie.

When I arrived at the tower, there was Alyssa leaning on her bike, grinning and pretending she'd been waiting for hours. She'd woken up early and was going to climb the tower with me even though she didn't want to. That's a true friend. I was really excited to see her, until I looked up. The tower suddenly looked enormous. It blotted out the egg yolk sun and threw its long shadow over the entire block. Still, I couldn't back down, not with Alyssa there.

We started up the narrow ladder. At first, it wasn't too

bad. As we got higher, though, Alyssa started to mutter that I was crazy. Pretty soon, she was saying it about every ten steps and her voice got more and more shaky.

"Make sure you don't look down!" I told her. So of course, I looked down. Right away my head got dizzy. My stomach felt like it had broken loose from my body and was hurtling back to the ground. That was when it occurred to me—Leo must have used a stunt double in the movie. He was probably never more than five feet off the ground. The director wouldn't have risked having his star slip and fall to his death. That director was a smart man.

I kept expecting Alyssa to give up and start back down the ladder, but she didn't. We made it to the walkway and collapsed, our legs shaking like Jell-O. Alyssa limply punched me on the arm.

"You're completely n-n-nuts," she said through chattering teeth.

We finally dragged ourselves up and sat with our legs hanging through the metal railing. Medford lay spread out below us like a toy city, with little dollhouses and windup cars. A tiny freight train chugged by on the tracks below us, tooting its tinny horn. We watched for a while, and then Alyssa turned to me, grinning, and told me I was brilliant.

We ate granola bars and watched ant people scurrying along the sidewalks. Medford suddenly looked small, surrounded by so much wide blue sky. From way up there, the horizon looked so close and I knew Hollywood lay just beyond it, right around the corner, waiting for me to take the big leap when I was ready.

When it was time to climb back down, Alyssa took one glance over the edge and had a meltdown. "You are a nut job!" she screamed at me. "Why did you drag me up here? We are both going to DIE!"

I kind of wanted to have a meltdown, too. Looking out at the horizon was great. Looking straight down the skinny ladder where we had to go made me want to throw up. I tried to act calm, though, since the whole thing *had* been my idea. That first step was the hardest. My legs went shaky and my palms were sweating so badly I was afraid they would slip right off the rungs.

Alyssa never said another word on the way down; she just moaned every now and then. When we reached the bottom, she collapsed on the ground and kissed the side-walk. I thought she was mad at me when she grabbed me and started screaming, but then she yelled that it was the most awesome thing she had ever done and she was never doing it again.

I think one day I'll make a movie about my growing-up years. I'll definitely have a water tower scene. It gives me a funny feeling, though, to think about casting girls to play Alyssa and me. It seems like *we* should play us. And then I realize, we kind of are. We're playing us right now in our own lives, which is sort of like one long movie with no rehearsals. And then I think about how one day my movie is going to end, so I should make every scene count. And I try to. I watch the amazing sunset. I listen when my mom goes on about chores and homework. I give my dad a hug. And then the phone rings or Derek calls me warthog or I get hungry, and I forget. I forget to pay attention.

Maybe *that's* why I really want to make movies—because then I can freeze all those great moments and replay them over and over. No matter what happens, in a movie Alyssa and I would always be this age, we would always be climbing the water tower and laughing at the old couple in Mickey D's, and she would always be my best friend.

5

I show Alyssa her scene so she can read it over. She never has many lines—it's mostly screaming and running—but she suddenly frowns. "Dude, we're shooting in the basement? Are you kidding?"

Oops. I meant to break that to her gently, but I forgot with the uproar about Lydia. Our basement is actually the perfect setting for a horror movie. It's dark and creepy and smells like an old dead person with really bad breath. My dad says we have mice, but I'm pretty sure they're rats, and the walls are always damp like they're sweating.

The problem is, it's a little too perfect for a horror movie. It's seriously scary. There's an old cistern, which is like an aboveground pool made out of concrete. It's way too disturbing to swim in, and there's no water in it anyway.

People used it for storing water before indoor plumbing got invented. Now I'm pretty sure it's a rat condo, so I keep my distance. The entire basement is lit with two bare bulbs plugged into the ceiling, so it's got lots of dark, shadowy corners and huge, invisible cobwebs that stick to your face and make you want to scream and run upstairs.

Before she agreed to be Mallory, Alyssa made me promise there wouldn't be any scenes in the basement.

"I've run out of locations," I tell her. "What do you expect after twenty-three scenes?"

"I'm not going in the basement," she says stubbornly, "and not the woods, either. I keep getting burrs in my hair, and last time I think I got poison ivy."

"Well, where am I supposed to put you, then?" I say crossly. I've already shot in every room in our house, the chicken coop twice, the woods three times, the road, the ditch. . . . But now that Lydia's coming over, I suddenly don't want to shoot in the basement, either. She might decide to tell kids at school how disgusting it is.

Alyssa shrugs. "We could run through the corn. We haven't done that before."

Just like that, she comes up with a brilliant idea. "That is perfect!" I shout, and Alyssa smiles modestly.

It's September, so the corn in the nearby field is way over our heads. It's already dried out, so it sounds shivery when it blows in the wind. I don't think Mr. Edgarton will mind. He owns the field, but he's nice and he was one of the picnic zombies. I figure he won't care if we knock down a few cornstalks for art's sake.

So I do a quick rewrite. Here's how the first part of the scene reads:

```
INT: MALLORY'S KITCHEN—DAY


Mallory opens the fridge door. Empty,
except for a bottle of ketchup and an
old sour cream container. She opens
the sour cream, but it's full of gross
globs of blue mold.
```

[My mother always has old containers of sour cream floating in the back of the fridge like handy horror movie props.]

```
She opens a cupboard, tips a box of
cereal upside down, and shakes it. A
few flakes fall out. The rest of the
cupboard is bare.


                MALLORY
               (worried)
    There's no food. What am I going
    to do?
```

She moves to the window, carefully
draws back the curtain, and peers
out. The yard is empty. She notices
the tall corn in the field across the
street. Her face lights up.

MALLORY
Lucky for me the farmers planted
their crops before they turned
into zombies.

But is it safe? She peers down the
road. Empty. No zombies in sight.

EXT: MALLORY'S FRONT YARD—CONTINUOUS

Mallory tiptoes onto the front porch,
then runs across the road.

Here's where I get stuck. How do I introduce the Lydia
zombie? It has to be good. Then I get a pretty genius idea
myself—the zombie will drive our old pickup down the road
and squeal to a stop near Mallory. Of course, it would have
to be my dad doing the driving. If I shoot it right, the reflec-
tions off the windshield from the sun will hide who's really
driving. Then I can cut away to a shot of Alyssa's horrified

face. The next shot would be Lydia getting out of the truck like she's doing the driving.

I'm excited at the thought of using my first-ever stunt car. Now I just need to convince my stunt driver.

My dad reads over the scene and purses his lips.

"I don't need a gaffer anymore," I tell him. "But I really want you to help us today, so I thought this would be perfect." I give him my pleading, fragile self-esteem eyes.

Finally, he smiles. "Sure, why not? It's not like we live on a major freeway."

"Thanks, Dad!"

The rest of the script will mostly be Lydia chasing Alyssa through the corn and Alyssa screaming, but I have to come up with an ending. Mallory always kills the zombies that chase her, and it's always with a different weapon—that's a signature calling card of my movie. She killed all the picnic zombies by tricking them into falling into the pond in our backyard. Zombies can't swim, so they all drowned. (Hey, it's my movie, so I make the rules. If I say zombies sink like rocks, then that's what they do. Movies are so much better than real life.)

Luckily for me, Derek has a toy weapon arsenal that would equip an army. So far, Mallory's weapons have included pistols, machine guns, a knife, a sword, rope, a wrench, poisonous plants, rat poison, the lawn mower, a sharp stick, and a can opener, among others.

I try to think what might be in the field that Mallory could use. She's already killed a zombie with a large rock, so that's no good, and ears of corn hardly sound lethal. Then I have my second inspiration of the day—Mallory can jump in the pickup truck and run the zombie down.

My dad balks at the idea, but I finally convince him by explaining exactly how we'll do it. Using the right camera angle, it will be easy to make it look like the pickup hits Lydia without actually running into her. By then, there are only ten minutes left before Lydia is supposed to arrive, and I still have lots to do. Take the kitchen scene, for instance. The entire fridge has to be cleaned out, so I get Alyssa working on that. The food also has to be pulled out of the cupboard, and I need an empty cereal box. All our boxes are pretty full, so I grab a gallon freezer bag and dump my mother's organic Puffed Brown Rice Crisps into it. Then I put a couple little crispies back in the box so they can fall out when Mallory shakes it.

I hear the crunch of gravel outside, and my stomach does a one-eighty flip. My zombie has arrived.

6

Sometimes people ask me why I'm making a zombie movie when I'm not even allowed to watch them. (My parents are movie Nazis and won't let me see R-rated movies, even though I've explained a million times that they're an important part of my professional development.)

The reason is real simple, and it's called Bad Acting. Nothing ruins a movie faster. Alyssa's pretty good, but most of my actors have never stood in front of a camera before, and let's just say they're not exactly ready for prime time. But even the world's worst actors can hold out their arms, roll their eyes, and moan.

That's why I feel okay casting Lydia as a zombie even though I don't know if she can act. And if anyone knows how to make noise, she does. Lydia doesn't even ring the doorbell; she just sticks her head in the door, sings out "Hello!" and waltzes in. You have to admire her nerve.

"Do I look like a zombie?" She pirouettes and makes a zombie face. Actually, she looks like a fashionable zombie. She's wearing torn jeans stuffed into black boots, and a T-shirt that's ragged in all the right places and probably cost a fortune. She's got on black lipstick and lots of dark eye makeup, which looks good on her, as I'm sure she knows. A few drops of fake blood ooze like tears from her eyes. I'm a little impressed. Most of my zombies don't show up ready for action.

"That's great!" I practically shout. It's amazing how loud people make you feel like you have to be loud, too. I've got nothing on Alyssa, though. She actually screams when she sees Lydia.

"Look at you! It's perfect! You are a total zombie. You're going to be the best zombie in the movie!"

Okay, that's going a little far. My dad scared Alyssa for real the day he played a zombie. We ripped up an old T-shirt and dripped fake blood all over him and smeared it all over his face. Then he agreed to mix baking soda and cola in his mouth, which made him foam up like a rabid dog.

So there was my dad, charging after Alyssa through the woods at dusk, bloody and gruesome, foaming at the mouth and making vomiting noises, which I think were real because of the baking soda and cola, which he said was the nastiest thing he'd drunk since college. Alyssa went screaming like a banshee and never stopped until she got back to our house. She said she didn't hear me call "cut," even though I yelled it about twenty times. All the running made her tired and she didn't want to go back into the woods again. Luckily that first take was amazing.

I doubt Lydia will be able to top that, but I swallow the thought. "Okay, here's the scene. Read it over and see what you think." I pretend to be busy, but I'm nervously watching Lydia.

"Oh, cool, I get to drive a car!" she screeches.

My dad walks in and jingles the car keys. "Famous actresses never do their own stunts. That's why they have underpaid stuntmen."

"Okay, let's get started," I say nervously, because I'm afraid my dad will say something embarrassing if he keeps talking.

We shoot the kitchen scene first. It goes fine, except Alyssa is self-conscious with Lydia watching and keeps cracking up when she's supposed to look worried about not having food. We finally get it, I grab a quick shot of her peeking out the window, and then we move outside—it's time for Lydia's big scene.

My dad revs up our old pickup, which is a perfect zombiemobile. It's a sun-fried blue Chevy splotched with rust, and the engine chugs like it's been raised from the dead a few times.

Just then, I hear Lydia scream, "That is so gross!"

She and Alyssa are laughing and staring at something on the ground. I get a funny feeling in the pit of my stomach as one of my mother's hens waddles away.

"It pooped!" Lydia announces. "I just saw a hen poop. This brown stuff squirted out of its butt onto the ground...." By then they're both laughing really hard. Lydia picks up a stick and pretends to flick the poop at Alyssa, who runs away screaming.

My dad gives me a look, like *Good luck with this*, and starts backing up the truck.

"Why do you guys have chickens?" Lydia asks. She's staring at them like they're alien life-forms.

"My mom raises organic chickens for upscale restaurants in the city." I try to put the best spin on it. "Have you ever eaten at Burberry's? They use her chickens and her eggs." Burberry's is the fanciest restaurant I can think of.

"Chickens are weird," Lydia announces. "And that poop *stinks*." She pinches her nose.

I decide to ignore the poop. Hopefully Lydia will forget about it with the excitement of her upcoming scene. I set my camera on its tripod, focus my shot, and shout, *"Action!"* Right on cue, my dad drives like a maniac zombie down the road. The pickup is supposed to squeal to a stop right next to Mallory. This goes perfectly. I stand behind Alyssa so the pickup is racing toward her and the camera. I shoot from a low angle so I don't even see the windshield, just the huge front grille barreling toward us. At the last second,

Alyssa jumps out of the way. It's definitely one of my best action sequences.

Finally it's Lydia's turn. She jumps into the pickup and I instruct her to kick open the door, jump out, and give a zombieish moan. I set up the camera and shout, "Action!"

The pickup door opens, barely, and I hear giggling. Lydia pokes out her head. "I tried to kick it and I missed! Can we do it again?"

"Sure," I call. We do two more takes. By the third, I start to get a terrible sinking feeling in my stomach. What happens next plays out more like a bad movie scene than real life, kind of like this:

EXT: COUNTRY ROAD—DAY

Lydia jumps out of the truck and ROARS like a demented lion. Lydia and Alyssa shriek with laughter. The director laughs, too.

                    DIRECTOR
     Ha-ha! Cut! Maybe less roaring.
     I think zombies moan more than
     roar.

                    LYDIA
     Got it. More moaning.

Lydia climbs into the pickup, swinging her hips and SNAPPING her fingers. Alyssa and the director laugh on cue.

Lydia jumps out of the car. She waves her arms and YOWLS like a rabid cat in heat. She and Alyssa collapse in the road, laughing. The director laughs, too, but not as much.

> DIRECTOR
> That's great. Once more, no laughing this time. Alyssa, you have to look afraid.

Alyssa starts to yowl, too. She and Lydia yowl a duet, waving their arms in the air.

> LYDIA
> How's that, Mrs. Director?

> DIRECTOR
> Uh, perfect. Let's shoot it again.

                    LYDIA
We should run through the
corn now!

                    ALYSSA
Yeah!

                    DIRECTOR
We'll do that as soon as we—

                    LYDIA
Here, shoot this!

Lydia barrels into the corn, SHOUTING
and waving her arms. Alyssa runs
after her.

                    ALYSSA
I'm a zombie, I'm a zombie! I
always wanted to be a zombie!

                    DIRECTOR
Uh, guys?

Loud SHUSHING noises, then SILENCE.
The corn CREAKS in the breeze. A

stifled GIGGLE. Loud SIGH from the
director.

> DIRECTOR
> Okay, I guess we can shoot in the
> corn. We'll just get this other
> shot later.

The corn scenes don't go much better. Lydia reminds me of the chickens. She doesn't understand about camera angles or hitting her mark (which means stopping where I tell her to so she doesn't end up off camera). She doesn't seem to really get what *Action* and *Cut* mean, either. I explain things for the third time.

Lydia earnestly nods. "I keep forgetting to stop! I just love running through the corn and screaming. Don't worry, Mrs. Director. This time I'm going to get it right."

She salutes me. Alyssa snickers.

"You're not supposed to laugh when you're running, Alyssa!" I bark, sharper than I mean to. But she's starting to bug me. This is Lydia's first time, but Alyssa knows better.

"I'm sick of being Mallory," she whines. "I want to be a zombie. They have more fun."

"Zombies have all the fun," Lydia agrees. "I think it would be cool to be a zombie and go around biting people's heads off."

Lydia grabs an ear of corn and rips it apart like a crazy woman. She tries to bite it, but the corn is hard, so she spits it out and says, "Bleah."

It's funny, but I'm not in the mood to laugh. Alyssa grabs an ear of corn and copies Lydia exactly, and this I find hugely annoying.

"Zombies don't bite people's heads off," I mutter, but they're already running away, screaming and ripping up corn. I can hear cornstalks crunching and trails of breathless laughter. A part of me wants to grab an ear of corn, run after them, and forget about the movie. But I'm the director. They're supposed to be doing what I tell them to do. And the shots of the pickup looked great, so I don't want the day to be a bust.

I trail after them with my camera. The corn is so tall and thick I can only see a couple of feet in front of me.

"I'm lost!" Lydia screams off to my left somewhere. "Alyssa, where are you?"

"I'm here!" Alyssa yells, somewhere off to my right.

"I'm here," I call, trying to get into the spirit of things.

"Marco!" Lydia bawls at the top of her lungs.

"Polo!" Alyssa shrieks back.

"Marco!"

"Polo!"

I call Polo, too, but it's clear they're only trying to find each other. I've become the third wheel, the pain-in-the-butt director they have to run away from. Resentment simmers inside me. I didn't expect much from Lydia, but Alyssa's behavior feels like treachery. They finally find each other, and I manage to find them.

"That was *so* scary," Lydia says, although she's clearly not afraid at all.

"We could get lost and die out here!" Alyssa squeals. "They wouldn't find our bones until next year!"

I roll my eyes. "The farmers harvest their corn in October. You'd barely be decomposed by then."

Alyssa shrugs. "Whatever."

I smile and try to take control of the situation. "Okay, let's shoot it once more. I just need you guys to run by the camera a few times, only do it in frame this time."

Lydia glances at Alyssa, and, just like that, I can tell neither of them wants to work on my movie anymore. Lydia groans. "I am so tired. Is there anything to drink? I did way too much running."

"Too bad I don't have any of it on camera," I mutter.

Lydia stares up at the sky. "Where, exactly, is your house?"

I glance around, but the corn towers over us—acres and acres of corn. We've done so much running I've lost all sense of direction. I jump up and down, and then we're all jumping up and down, but it doesn't do any good.

We grin at one another because it's kind of funny that

we're actually lost in a cornfield. It will make a great story at school on Monday morning. Who knows? After Lydia gets done telling it, maybe the whole seventh-grade class will want to be zombies in my movie. I feel cheered.

"I know," I say. "You two get on your hands and knees, and I'll climb on your backs and see if I can see anything."

"You're the shortest," Lydia says.

"I'll be the lightest," I explain.

Lydia sticks out her lower lip. "Are you calling me fat?"

Now, Lydia never means what she says. It's all about getting laughs. If I were smart, I'd say something like, *Yeah, fatty,* and she would probably snicker. But I'm still a little nervous and resentful, so I say, "Uh, no, you're not fat," which is pathetic and not funny at all.

"Well, I'm tallest," she says, "so you two get down and I'll look."

She and Alyssa are the same height, but Alyssa hits the ground like a dropped brick, so I get down, too. Lydia climbs on, and she's a lot heavier than she looks. She can't just look and hop off; she has to do a little jig up there like she's losing her balance, digging her heel into my spine. And she didn't bother to take her boots off, so now I've got dirty footprints on my back.

"See anything?" I call.

"Nada. Corn's too tall."

Well, Mr. Edgarton did say it was a bumper crop this

year. A last dig in the spine and Lydia jumps down. She snaps her fingers. "I know. You ladies give me a leg up and I'll stand on your shoulders. That should work."

"I'm the lightest," I point out. "I should climb up."

Lydia rolls her eyes. "Fine."

There's so much giggling and protesting that it takes me ten minutes to wriggle onto their shoulders. I didn't want to leave my camera on the ground, where they might step on it, so I'm still holding it in one hand. It bangs against their heads as I climb up and they think I'm doing it on purpose, but I'm not. Not really.

"Are you taking a siesta up there, or what?" Lydia bellows, because I'm still crouching on their shoulders, hanging on to their heads. I don't really want to stand up, because I already feel pretty wobbly. I make them grab on to my legs, and then I finally raise myself up. Sure enough, I see our house and it's farther away than I thought.

"I see it," I call, pointing in the distance. "It's over there...."

I hear muted giggling, then all of a sudden Lydia and Alyssa start staggering as if I'm too heavy.

"Aaaagh!" Lydia shouts. "You're mutilating my shoulder!"

"We can't hold you up!" Alyssa calls. "Jump!"

There's no way I'm jumping down from that height. I try to crouch, but Lydia lets go of my leg and then Alyssa stumbles like she tripped. I go flying off their shoulders

48

and land hard on the ground, and the corn really doesn't cushion my fall at all.

"I think we killed her," Lydia says. They both come over and lift the hair off my face, trying not to giggle, but I slap their hands away and roll over, groaning.

"Are you okay?" Alyssa's voice drips with fake concern. "I tripped," she proclaims in her worst actor's voice.

"You did not," I say. "You did it on purpose."

"Ooooh, someone's mad," Lydia says. "Don't get mad, Kate. Get even."

It takes all my self-control not to tell her to buzz off. I manage a smile and say, "Oh, I will," in a passably evil voice, but somehow it's not funny. This only makes me feel worse.

"I'm going to die if I don't have something to drink, like, *immediately*," Lydia declares. "Last one to the house is a freakin' zombie."

She takes off running and Alyssa starts after her, then pauses to glance back at me.

"You okay?"

I nod, pulling twigs out of my hair.

"Come on, then!"

She bolts after Lydia. I sit up and clean off my camera, which fell in the dirt. It took me a long time to earn enough money to buy my camera. I spent an entire summer baby-sitting the neighbors' kids and cleaning out the chicken coop, plus I had to use birthday and Christmas money. It's like my baby. I clean it and fuss over it, and I probably have way too many photos of me posing with it. Alyssa knows all this. I'm always reminding her that electronics break easily and we need to be careful with it, but she still let it drop on the ground without a second thought. This bothers me more than my own tumble.

I slowly stand up and brush myself off. No broken bones, anyway. I limp back toward the house, wondering if any famous directors ever let loose with a few tears when they had a really bad day on the set, but somehow it's hard to imagine Steven Spielberg crying.

7

Lydia ends up getting a ride home with Alyssa at the end of the day, so I don't get a chance to ask Alyssa about her strange behavior.

After they leave, my dad finds me in the kitchen. "How did it go?"

I don't feel like explaining how the day was a major disaster, so I just mumble, "Fine."

"You have footprints on your back."

I sigh. "Yeah, I know."

"Okay, then. As long as you know." My father drums his fingers on the counter, looking distracted. "Uh, where's your mother?"

"I think she's in the chicken coop."

He peers outside. "Well, I've got some work to do. I'll be in the den."

My mother made chocolate chip cookies while we were outside shooting. Alyssa and Lydia each had three before they left. I ate three, too, but I decide one more won't hurt. There's nothing like warm, gooey chocolate chip cookies melting in your mouth to make you feel better.

As I head for my bedroom, I pass the den. It's a small room with old wooden floors that my dad took over as his home office. He usually closes the door when he's working, but today it's open. I glance inside and see why. Wilma is curled up on a chair, snoozing. She has a talent for pushing open doors that aren't quite latched and making herself comfortable. My dad is sitting with his back to me at his desk, on the phone as usual. The way he's talking sounds funny, though. Not businesslike.

"It's getting hard to keep this a secret." His voice is low, almost a murmur. "It's all getting very complicated." He chuckles. "I know. Me, too. Have I told you lately how much I—"

Wilma picks this moment to notice me. She jumps off the chair, knocking over a stack of papers. My dad twists in his seat and spots me, frozen, in the doorway.

It's too late to flee, so I push open the door and march in, like I was planning on visiting him all along. I draw near his desk. How can I find out who he's talking to? I'm pretty sure it isn't his boss. "Uh, Dad, I was wondering if you could help me with something."

It sounds suitably vague. My brain is cranking hard, trying to figure out what he can help me with. It doesn't matter, because my dad frowns like the answer is no.

"Not now, Kate! Haven't I told you to knock first before you come in?"

He looks flustered, then tries to smile, not quite meeting my gaze. "Ask me a little later, okay? I'm kind of busy right now."

I shrug. "Okay."

He's holding the phone, waiting for me to leave. I trudge out and hear the door firmly click shut behind me.

"It's the weekend," I mutter to Wilma as I scratch her ears. "Why is he working on a Saturday? And what is he keeping secret?"

If this were a movie, Wilma would be a talking dog and tell me everything she heard while my dad was on the phone. It's not, though, so she just licks my hand.

As I think about his strange behavior, it hits me with a nasty jolt that my dad has been holing up in the den and talking on the phone a lot lately. And he's called my mother from the office several times and told her he has to work late. I never gave it a second thought. Now I wonder. What is he really doing, and who is he talking to?

I don't want to think about why he's acting this way.

My dad would never do that, I tell myself, but I can't bring myself to say what *that* is.

I watch him at dinner that night as he talks to Derek about baseball. He catches my eye and smiles at me.

"What do you think, Kate? Will the Cubs go all the way next year?"

"Nah," I answer. "Not a chance."

"Yes they will!" Derek bellows. He's a big Chicago Cubs fan.

"You say that every year," I point out.

My dad laughs and smiles at my mother. Somehow, I feel relieved. He couldn't act so normal with us if he was doing something wrong. Those few sentences I heard could have been about anything.

Plus, I have plenty of other things to worry about, like Alyssa. She calls my cell phone later that night.

"Sorry about today," she says right away. "I know we were acting like idiots."

"Yeah, you kind of were," I say, trying to keep it light.

"It's just, I sort of feel sorry for Lydia. When we were in the park the other night, she was talking about her parents' divorce. I guess her dad had a midlife crisis or something. Now her mom is always saying nasty things about him and how he's a lowlife." Alyssa pauses. "And I guess he kind of is because he had a girlfriend—that's why they divorced. Lydia can't stand her. And now her sister, Shannon, is in high school, and I guess she's crawling out her window and running around every night drinking with her friends."

My jaw drops open. "She told you all that?"

"Yeah, everybody left to go shoot hoops, but we stayed and talked. Can you believe that? I never thought of Lydia Merritt having problems."

"Yeah, she always seems so . . . loud, like everything's great."

"Anyway, I wanted to make sure she had fun, you know?"

I nod, then I realize she can't see me. "You should have told me."

"Well, she asked me not to say anything, so you have to promise not to tell anyone."

"You know I won't." My head is spinning from so much information. It all makes sense now. I'm hugely relieved, but I'm also a little jealous. Alyssa probably told Lydia about her parents' divorce, too. It's like she and Lydia share a bond now. Still, I feel sorry for Lydia. It seems like every year more and more kids end up with divorced parents.

I feel another twinge of anxiety as I think of my own parents. What, exactly, does a midlife crisis look like? My dad's phone conversation replays in my head. What is getting too complicated in his life? Could my parents' marriage be crumbling in front of me and I don't even realize it?

"Was Lydia surprised about the divorce?" I ask casually. "I mean, did she know they had problems?"

"It was a total shock. She said everything seemed fine. Her dad acted completely normal. And then one day, guess what, kids? We're getting divorced."

"That's tough."

"Yeah." Alyssa's voice is subdued.

Is my dad's strange behavior a warning sign? I suddenly remember other things, too, like the way he swears under his breath after he steps in chicken poop. And the way he rolls his eyes at some of my mom's organic food when he thinks no one is looking. Is he sorry we moved to the country? Is he feeling trapped? My mom always used to look so pretty in her high heels and lipstick. Now she looks like a frumpy farmer's wife.

And what about my mother? Is her crazy chicken farm idea just a midlife crisis? Does she ever wish she had married a big, strapping outdoors type instead of a business manager with glasses and thinning hair? She's always running down the road to talk to Mr. Cunningham. He has a real farm with cows and chickens and horses. He's big and strong and still has lots of hair. Maybe my mom is the one who feels trapped.

I feel dizzy just thinking about it.

"Well, I'll see you Monday at school," Alyssa says.

"Yeah, thanks for calling."

As I hang up, a nervous flutter starts in my stomach. I never gave my parents' marriage a second thought before today. What if it's a slow freight train about to head off a cliff? And what about Lydia and Alyssa? If we still lived in town, I would have been at the park that night, too. I could have listened to Lydia and been sympathetic. It would have been the three of us having fun together today instead of me running around clueless in the corn.

I start getting mad just thinking about it. My mother ripped up our family by the roots and transplanted us to the middle of nowhere, just because she got some crazy idea into her head about raising chickens. She never thought about how it might affect me, Dad, and Derek. When I was young, she was always telling me to share and not be selfish, and to think of others. It seems like maybe she forgot her own advice.

Alyssa is especially nice at school on Monday. Near the end of the day, when we're at our lockers, she gives me a photo of a hen with glowing red eyes. Her dad is a graphic designer, so I'm guessing he Photoshopped it on his computer.

"It's perfect," I tell her. "I wish I could get their eyes to do that in my movie."

I hang it up in my locker as Lizzy Chang and Mimi Reynolds hurry over.

"Did you hear?" Mimi asks. "Mr. Cantrell says the winter musical is going to be *Annie*. All the girls in choir say they're trying out."

"And Mr. Cantrell says he's already ordered a red wig from New York for the star to wear," Lizzy chimes in.

Singing is definitely not one of my talents. I'm only allowed in choir class because it doesn't require an audition. "Are you guys trying out?" I ask them.

"No way!" They squeal so loudly that I know they'll be trying out for sure.

Both Mimi and Lizzy have been zombies in my movie. Mimi has a soft voice and her zombie moaning sounded more like someone with a toothache, but she had a great death scene (the infamous riding mower). Lizzy hid under a bed and Mallory killed her by using an extralong sword and plunging it right through the mattress. Derek charged me five dollars to rent his collapsible sword, but it was worth it. When Alyssa plunged the sword into the bed, the tip popped a thin plastic bag full of blood hidden under the blanket. The white sheet turned bloodred. It was amazing. Lizzy pointed out that blood wouldn't seep upward (everybody's an expert), but I explained to her that zombie blood does.

"Are you going to try out for *Annie*?" Lizzy asks Alyssa. She knows better than to ask if I'm trying out for a singing part.

"You should," I encourage Alyssa. "You'd be awesome." She's a little pitchy when she sings, but hey, she's a lot better than me.

"Mrs. Director, I'm ready for my close-up!"

Lydia waltzes up, surrounded by her usual group of hangers-on. I'm flattered that she's singled me out. Sara

Gonzalez and Emily Foster stare at me like they're trying to decide if I'm suddenly part of their gang. I can't think of a single witty comeback, so I just smile and say, "Hey, Lydia."

I know, lame.

Alyssa does better. "Heya, zombie," she says in a carefully careless voice. "Eaten any corn lately?"

We all laugh, and then Lydia turns to her fan club. "Did I tell you guys I was in a zombie movie this weekend? No lie. You should have seen me."

And just that fast, Alyssa whips out her cell phone and shows them a photo of Lydia, which I didn't even know she'd taken. Sara and Emily grab the phone from each other and scream. Other girls are already edging toward our circle, wanting to be part of the action.

"Seriously," Lydia goes on, "we were running through this huge cornfield for, like, an hour, and Mrs. Director here was screaming 'Cut! Cut! You're not being zombie enough,' and making us reshoot twenty times. We got totally lost in the corn, just running around in circles, and finally Mrs. Director stood on our shoulders, and it turns out she's made out of concrete. I think my shoulder's still dislocated...."

"And then you dropped me into the corn and broke my neck," I add, and Sara and Emily laugh. The most I got them to redo a scene was three times, but that's okay. All the girls are grinning. Any moment, they're going to start begging me to be zombies.

"Oh, and you won't believe this," Lydia says. "I actually saw a chicken poop. It was the grossest thing."

Wha-a-a? I didn't see that one coming. Warning bells start clanging in my head.

"A *chicken*?" Sara repeats, like it's a word from a foreign language.

"Her mom's got a hundred chickens running all over the place, and they're *not* exactly what you would call house-trained, ladies." Lydia pauses for effect. "One almost pooped on my boots. I was like, don't you poop on my boot, Mr. Chicken, or I'll kick you over the garage...."

Everyone's laughing, but Sara and Emily are staring at me like I'm strange. I try to cut Lydia off, but it's like trying to dam the Mississippi River with a stick.

"They're organic," I say, because at least organic is cool.

"Organic poop," Lydia says, and I wish she would shut up, or go back to talking about my movie. "So this one lets it rip and, I'm not kidding, this brown stuff squirts out and almost hits me...."

Squeals of delighted disgust all around.

Lydia wasn't anywhere near the chicken, and it's a Mrs. Chicken, not a Mr., and my mother only has fifty hens right now, not one hundred, but I know this is all totally beside the point.

"That is so gross," Emily says. "Do you ever step in the poop, Kate?"

The truth is it's hard *not* to step in it because the hens do poop pretty much wherever they want. My dad needs to get the outdoor pen finished, quick. I shake my head. "It's not that bad. . . ."

"You should see their dog, Wilma," Alyssa pipes up. "She's like a poop-eating machine. She *loves* to eat chicken poop. And she likes to roll in it, too." Alyssa beams as everyone goes into another round of laughing, squealing disbelief. There are probably ten girls surrounding us now, and they're all darting glances my way, relieved, no doubt, that they're not me. "And her little brother puts dried poop in his slingshot and tries to *hit* us with it!"

Unfortunately this is all true. Eating and rolling in poop seem to be Wilma's two favorite pastimes. My brother only shot poop at us once, though, and he got in big-time trouble for it.

"Oh, yeah," I say weakly, "it's *so* disgusting." I'm laughing, but inside I'm cringing because everyone in my family sounds like a weirdo now, including me. Alyssa should have known better and kept her mouth shut, but she's trying to score points with Lydia's gang. Sadly it seems to be working. They're all making jokes about rolling in poop. It's like we're six years old again, which just shows the power of poop, I guess. It's funny at any age.

Nobody asks me if they can be in my zombie movie.

Lydia says, "Here comes Margaret." Then she does an

exaggerated wave. "Hi, Margaret!" while Sara and Emily giggle under their breath.

"Hi." Margaret beams at us. "Hi, Kate." She kind of ducks her head and grins, and I thank God that I'm not as socially hopeless as Margaret. I may not be Lydia Merritt, but I know not to grin so much, especially with a mouthful of teeth like hers.

A funny thing about Margaret—she always singles me out. Margaret Yorkel has wanted to be my friend ever since I went to her third-grade birthday party (it was just me, Margaret, and her sister), and I've been trying *not* to be her friend ever since. I don't have anything against her, but it's just a cold, hard fact—being friends with Margaret would be the social kiss of death.

Some days I feel sorry for Margaret and other days I want to shake her. Mostly I'd love to give her a makeover. Now, if I had bright red hair like that, I'd dye it brunette. I'd buy concealer for the freckles and I'd definitely look into contacts. She has pretty blue eyes, but you can't see them behind her thick lenses. And wouldn't you think her parents could spring for some braces? If it were me, I'd lock myself in the bathroom until my parents sold the family jewels or my little brother—whatever it took to throw some braces on my teeth, pronto.

I grab a book out of my locker. My social stock is sinking by the second, and the last thing I need is Margaret hanging around. "Gotta go!" I give a quick wave and head down the hallway. Alyssa doesn't follow, even though we usually walk to business ed class together. That's fine, because I don't want to hear her scratchy, out-of-pitch voice anyway.

Alyssa ends up being late to class. She slips in after the bell rings and smiles at the teacher. Mrs. Chapman is a dour, gray-haired, old-school feminist who always talks about how there used to only be two jobs open to women—nursing and teaching. Men got to have all the other jobs. Then women of her generation finally cracked the glass ceiling, and now we girls have to keep up the fight.

Sometimes Mrs. Chapman will lower her voice and tell us there's even a glass ceiling at our school. She whispers that everyone with power is pale, male, and stale. We all titter and wonder if she's talking about the principal, Mr. Safire, who's actually pretty tan because he plays golf on the weekends, and his breath isn't nearly as stale as Mrs. Chapman's.

I wait for Mrs. Chapman to give Alyssa a detention because she hates it when people show up late, but she actually *smiles* at her.

"As you all know, this is the start of National Career Week," Mrs. Chapman announces. We all look at one another with blank faces. National Career Week?

"Many of your mothers have exciting careers today, largely due to the efforts of the women of my generation,"

Mrs. Chapman goes on. "We fought the battles with blood, sweat, and tears. And now your mothers stand on our shoulders, carrying the torch."

Mrs. Chapman's eyes look misty. Someone snickers, and she frowns and raps her ruler on the desk. "Alyssa Jensen's mother has graciously agreed to come in today and talk with us about her career and how she got started in it."

The door opens and Mrs. Jensen slips in. She's dressed like a businesswoman: black pantsuit, nice blouse, high-heeled pumps. Just like my mother used to dress. I stare at Alyssa. She never told me her mother was coming in. Alyssa's cheeks are pink. She looks happy but nervous, because there's always the chance her mother will slip up and say something embarrassing. It's not likely with Mrs. Jensen, though. For a mom, she's pretty hip. She thanks Mrs. Chapman and then perches on the edge of the desk like a bright-eyed bird.

Mrs. Jensen tells us about her job on the marketing team for a high-end cosmetics firm and how she travels all over the country trying to get their brand into department stores. I already knew this, but it's interesting to hear about it anyway. She gets a big round of applause at the end.

Alyssa's mother suddenly whips out a pink lacy-edged shopping bag and announces she's got free makeup samples for everyone. That's when the class goes nuts. All the girls jump up and crowd around her. Lydia is the loudest of all. The boys look glum except for Steve Bascombe, who's into

Goth and wears black eyeliner. They look happier after Mrs. Jensen announces she has aftershave for them, even though none of them actually shaves yet.

"Can I have two lip glosses?" Lydia asks right away.

"Sure." Alyssa has already taken over the pink bag and is handing out cosmetics to all the girls. Her mother looks on and beams, the picture of professional poise.

Alyssa lets Lydia pick her second lip gloss before I even get my first one. By the time I reach the front of the line, all that's left is a brown shade called Raisin the Roof. When we return to our seats, Lydia sits next to Alyssa.

"That is so cool your mom sells makeup," I overhear Lydia say. "My mother sells houses." She rolls her eyes to show that houses are pretty useless compared with makeup.

Mrs. Chapman claps her hands and tells us never to forget what a difference we can make and that we have to keep fighting because the struggle isn't over yet. Alyssa's mother looks slightly confused at this, but she smiles and thanks us for letting her come in. I think of my own mother stomping around in her big, dirty boots and stained work clothes, mucking out the chicken crap. She loves what she's doing, I tell myself loyally, but I can't help thinking it's too bad she doesn't love selling cosmetics or jewelry or iPads.

After school, I have an appointment with the orthodontist. My teeth aren't nearly as crooked as Margaret's, but my parents have decided that I need braces. I don't mind too much, because most of the kids in school have them and I get to pick the color of the wires, which I've decided will be purple. The orthodontist's name is Dr. Payne. The first time I met him, when they took X-rays of my teeth, he started joking about his name right away. "Hi, I'm Dr. Payne. Terrible name for an orthodontist, isn't it? But don't worry, little lady, we specialize in painless orthodontics. So you get Dr. Payne, without the pain." He beamed at my mother and me. I politely laughed and wondered where my mother came up with this guy.

On this day, Dr. Payne is all business. He's tall and thin with stooped shoulders, like he's spent too many years bending over kids' mouths. He cranks me up superhigh on the chair, then starts asking questions while his rubber-gloved hands are poking and prodding inside my mouth. "You like school this year? Doing any sports? Getting good grades, I hope?"

"Aauurgh," I answer each time, which he seems to understand, because he nods and fires off another question. When it's finally over, my lips feel rubbery from all the pulling and stretching. I stare with horror in the mirror. Other people don't look bad in braces, but I look repulsive. All that shiny metal grinning freakishly back at me. Alyssa is lucky; her teeth are straight and she doesn't need braces. I touch the bands with my tongue, wishing I could rip them off.

"They look great," my mother says in her fake hearty voice. I brush past her and hurry out to the car. At least they don't hurt too bad. I had heard that braces could be painful, but I guess I have a pretty tough mouth.

When my mother stops at the grocery store, I pretend I'm sleeping so I don't have to go inside with her. I spend the whole time staring at my mouth from every angle in the rearview mirror. I could be a zombie in my movie. People would scream with fright at the sight of me.

My mother finally returns with groceries, and I pretend to be asleep again.

As soon as we get home, she turns to me as if she knows

I'm fake sleeping. "Can you take all the groceries inside, please? I need to take care of a few things in the chicken coop."

"I have homework," I point out, my eyes still closed, but she's already out of the car, hurrying away. I sigh, then grab some bags and head for the house. As soon as I get inside, my cell phone rings. Alyssa. I'm not sure if I want to talk to her after she sold me out for a few laughs. But deep down, I have to admit it *was* pretty funny. I can see why Alyssa got carried away. Lydia is popular. That's the nearest thing to being a celebrity in our boring, suburban town where nobody famous ever steps foot. And it's hard to resist Lydia's personality—kind of like trying to stand firm in a tsunami without getting swept away.

In fact, I've noticed that Lydia has her own gravitational pull, like the sun. People get sucked in and then they're trapped. They keep revolving around her, too scared to break away and see what life might be like outside her mega-voltage. The tricky part is, Lydia only has one best friend—or at least one at a time. She switches about once a month. She and the chosen one are always together, hanging on each other, laughing a mile a minute—until the next month. Then Lydia gets bored and moves on, and the girl is left with a Lydia hangover, wondering what happened.

Still, the whole scene in the hallway left me looking pretty lame. So I answer the phone and just say, "Yeah?"

There's a pause on the other end. "Are you mad?"

"Why would I be mad?" I ask, even though we both know perfectly well why.

"You know. . . ." Alyssa's voice trails away. "After I told that story about Wilma, I wasn't sure if you minded me telling people. I guess I got carried away."

"You definitely got carried away." At this point I can stay mad at her or I can be gracious and let it go. I decide to let it go. "It's okay. I guess it was funny."

"I was nervous, too, about my mother giving her talk."

"Yeah, why didn't you tell me about that?"

"I thought I did tell you," Alyssa says hurriedly.

And I'm pretty sure that means she told Lydia instead. Then Alyssa launches into a long story about how Paul Corbett got caught trying to plug a toilet in the boys' bathroom and almost got suspended, but his mother called the school and threatened a lawsuit, so they decided to give him a warning instead.

"This officially qualifies Paul for the Kate Walden List of Morons," I tell her.

"That's probably the highest achievement of his life so far," Alyssa jokes.

"Hens are in the garage again!" Derek suddenly shouts from the kitchen window.

I glance over and see two hens jump into the back of the car. In my rush, I left both the garage and the car door open. "Gotta go!" I tell Alyssa.

I dash outside. The hens love the garage because it's

shady and they can roost on the shelves. They peck and poop and make a huge mess, so we're under strict orders to keep the garage door closed until my dad finishes the outdoor pen.

Four chickens are throwing a party in the back of our Suburban. They're pecking away at the rest of the grocery bags like it's a feast. Four apples are already DOA, and I no longer have to worry about eating zucchini for dinner. Some other hens found the loaf of bread, carried it out of the car, ripped open the plastic bag, and are now chowing down as fast as they can.

They all freeze and stare at me with their beady eyes. It actually makes me pause. There's something spooky about a bunch of chickens staring at you. Then they all start clucking like something is hilarious and I quickly see why. The evil birds have pooped inside the car. Not in the garage on the concrete, where it would be easy to clean up. They've pooped all over the carpeting of my mother's seminew Suburban.

"That's it!" I shout. "You stupid birds are dead meat!" I chase them out of the garage and throw a chewed-up apple after them. Derek sees it through the window and tells our mother, so I get in trouble for leaving the car door open, letting the groceries get ruined, *and* throwing the apple. The fact that I'm stressed about my new braces doesn't seem to matter. I'm stuck cleaning up the poop *and* I'm grounded off TV for three days. Once again, the hens have outmaneuvered me.

My dad tells me my braces look fantastic and Derek says I look like Frankenstein's Bride, so I figure it's somewhere in between. By the end of dinner, my teeth are beginning to hurt. I go up to my room and stare at them again from every angle. I look like a baby now. A part of me wishes that Alyssa needed braces. It wouldn't be quite so bad if she were getting them, too. Of course, she has a perfect mouth to go along with her perfect hair. I practice smiles from every angle, but they're all horrible. It's depressing. I won't be able to smile for the next two years.

10

When I wake up the next morning, my mouth feels like every single tooth has been yanked out and glued back in. I have to force down lumpy oatmeal for breakfast because it's too painful to chew anything else. As I'm eating, I overhear my dad tell my mother he's going to be home late again. He waves as he heads out the door but doesn't notice when I don't wave back. I guess he's in a big hurry to get to the office.

If he has a secret, then why is he sharing it with a mystery person on the phone and not with us? I want to ask my mother what she thinks, but then I would have to tell her what I overheard. It would sound like I was spying on my dad, and it's probably all nothing anyway, so I should just stop thinking about it.

I beg to stay home, but my mother just hands me some pain reliever. Before I leave to catch the bus, she gives me an extra-big smile. "Have a great day today. I'll see you later, okay?" I swallow the aspirin, not really paying attention. Dr. Payne without the pain. What a load of chicken doo-doo.

By the time I reach school, the aspirin have kicked in and I can at least see straight. I hurry to my locker, hoping to slip in and out unnoticed.

"Kate, you got braces!" a familiar voice sings out behind me. Margaret Yorkel. "They look great!"

How did she see them? She must have X-ray vision because I'm sure I haven't smiled once. I wave without turning around and call out "Thanks!" As I hurry away, Paul Corbett yowls, "Kate, you got braces!" in his annoying falsetto. Now all the kids are looking up from their lockers, waiting to see what will happen next. And Margaret has dragged me into it just by calling my name.

"Hey, Margie, what're all those brown spots on your face—is that a skin disease?" One thing about Paul, he never gets tired of the same joke.

"They're freckles," Margaret answers.

I groan to myself. Margaret needs to learn *not* to answer—unless it's a quick, verbal kick in the jaw. That's all these boys understand. Now Blake Nash is grinning. He's worse than Paul.

"Hey, Margarine, can I connect the dots?" Blake gets out a marker and acts like he's going to draw on her face.

Margaret reminds me of some of my mother's chickens, the ones with nasty bald spots on their backs. My mother explained to me once how weird expressions like *henpecked* and *pecking order* and *rule the roost* got invented. Put a bunch of hens together and those clucking, mild-mannered birds will peck one another until their feathers fly, trying to figure out who's the head honcho hen. They'll keep pecking until they know everybody's place, right down to the bottom of the heap. Well, if Lydia Merritt is ruler of the roost, then Margaret Yorkel is definitely the Chicken Little of our seventh-grade class.

I listen to Blake and Paul, wishing there was a way to shut them up. But I know if I say anything, I'll become the next target. Those two are like pimply bulldogs. Once they grab hold of something, they don't let go, and I don't want to be their next victim. Just as I'm telling myself there's nothing I can do, Lydia waltzes over and grabs the pen from Blake's hand.

"Can I connect your zits, Nashville?" she says loudly. Everyone nearby laughs. We're all secretly glad to see Blake Nash get zinged. He flushes red.

"Ha-ha, Merritt," he mutters. He wisely keeps quiet after that. Blake knows he'll end up in shreds if he tries to take on Lydia.

She tosses the marker back to him. It bounces off his head before he can catch it, and everyone titters. Ouch. Blake Nash is suddenly having a bad day. I just hope he doesn't decide to take it out on Margaret the first chance he gets.

I slip into my seat in history class. Lydia put Blake in his place so easily. Of course, she's the MPG. She doesn't have to worry about her social standing or whether Blake will harass her—the things most kids have to worry about. Blake probably has a secret crush on her. Most of the boys do.

The funny thing is, sometimes Lydia makes fun of Margaret, too, although never to her face. We're all guilty of it. The red hair, the freckles, the glasses . . . she's a tempting target. But today, Lydia stood up for Margaret. Which Lydia is the real one?

It's too confusing to sort out, so I start thinking about the footage I shot of Lydia instead. I know the car shots look great, but after that I'm not so sure. Some really creative editing might save the scene. If I show Lydia a rough cut, maybe she'll get excited and agree to let me grab a few more shots. Maybe she'll forget about the hens and start talking about my movie again. I liked how everyone laughed at her stories, right up until she mentioned the poop.

I plan and plot all day and I'm feeling pretty good by the time business ed rolls around at the end of the afternoon. I sit next to Alyssa, and she hands me a lip gloss that's called Berried Alive, which is a lot prettier than Raisin the Roof. Just as I'm settling into my seat, feeling good about things, Mrs. Chapman walks through the door, followed by my mother.

At first I'm confused and I wonder if everything's okay. Then my mother waves at me, beaming like she's just jumped out of a magician's hat. My stomach does a hard flip and my heart starts to pound. She wouldn't, I think. She couldn't. I sink into my seat, my mind cranking furiously, trying to find a way to stop the train wreck that's about to happen.

At least my mother took off her work boots. She looks clean and pretty normal in blue jeans and a blouse and her good sneakers. She even did her hair and put on makeup. She doesn't look professional like Alyssa's mom, but at least she doesn't look like Farmer Bob.

"I didn't know your mother was coming," Alyssa whispers.

"Neither did I," I croak. I think back to my mother's cheery good-bye that morning. She must have been planning this as a surprise. Well, it worked, I'm surprised— although *shocked* might be a better word.

Then Mrs. Chapman claps her hands for quiet. "Class, I'd like to introduce Mrs. Jean Walden, Kate's mother. Mrs. Walden's career path has taken a very interesting twist lately. She's gone from business executive to entrepreneur. Does everyone know what that is? An entrepreneur is someone who has a vision and starts her own business, just like Mrs. Walden. As part of Career Week, she's here today to tell you about it."

As the class politely claps, I'm riveted to my seat, my face frozen in a glassy smile. My teeth start to ache again. My mother loves what she's doing, I remind myself. In fact, the day she quit her job she got so excited that she called our family together and marched us outside to the fire pit. She had piled up a bunch of skirts, some snarled pantyhose, and a few pairs of high heels (not her favorite ones, I noticed). She splashed gasoline on them, lit a match, and gave us a huge smile like she was about to light the Olympic flame.

The wind blew out the first match. And the second. Some of the gas must have evaporated by then because, after she finally got the pile lit, the pantyhose melted right away but the skirts just smoked a bit. My dad scratched his head. I knew he was adding up how much all those outfits cost, but he didn't want to spoil her big, triumphal moment. We applauded and tried to look happy.

My mother looks happy now as she thanks Mrs. Chapman. She's an entrepreneur—that sounds pretty cool. Maybe it won't be so bad, I tell myself.

My mother takes a deep breath. "I am a chicken farmer," she says dramatically.

I have to clamp shut my mouth to keep a groan from escaping. From the corner of my eye, I see Emily Foster glance at Lydia and then over at me.

"I used to be a manager at Sun Market Systems, which produces financial software for businesses. It was a good job, but I was starting to feel stuck in a rut. One of my passions is quality organic food. And my dream has always been to work with animals. So I decided to quit my job and raise organic chickens. I sell the meat and eggs to a natural foods chain and to a few high-end restaurants in the city."

My mother smiles and perches on the desk. "This has meant some big changes, as I'm sure Kate has told you." The entire class turns and looks at me. If only someone would play a prank and pull the fire alarm. No one does and my mother continues.

"I had to educate myself about raising chickens, everything from housing to chicken feed to processing."

Nathan Fremont raises his hand. "I thought you weren't allowed to have farm animals in town."

My mother nods. "You're not, but luckily we live outside town on an acreage."

Then Emily raises her hand. "Don't chickens poop a lot?" she asks in an overly sweet voice. A snigger runs through the room. Mrs. Chapman frowns at us.

"That's a very good question," my mother says brightly. "Disposal of animal waste is a problem in any farming operation. Luckily chicken manure makes excellent compost for gardens. And because our chickens are organic, their manure is organic, too. I have people stop and ask if they can buy manure from me."

My mother actually smiles happily as a titter goes around the classroom. In a crazed moment, I wonder if she's doing it on purpose. Maybe she was more upset by my zombie chicken script than I'd thought. But, no, she's clearly oblivious to the brewing tidal wave that's about to capsize my life.

"Chicken manure is very high in nitrogen, which is great for gardens. I used it in our garden as fertilizer last year, and we had a bumper crop of tomatoes."

"Crappy tomatoes," Blake Nash mutters under his breath, and that sets off another round of giggles.

Lydia raises her hand and I wish a flash flood would sweep through or a freak tornado would touch down, but nothing happens. I'm locked rigid in my seat, and my face feels hot enough to cook something on. I can't tell which hurts more, my mouth or my head.

"I saw one of your chickens poop." The blunt way Lydia announces it makes everyone laugh. "Let's just say it was . . . fragrant." She waves a hand in front of her nose and rolls her eyes.

My mother laughs along with the rest of the class. Alyssa, I notice, is laughing the loudest.

"Poop is poop," my mother says cheerfully. "Yes, it's smelly, but you get used to it. Kate and her brother help me clean up around the yard."

The looks I'm getting vary from amazed sympathy to sneers, depending on the looker. I can't sink any lower without disappearing underneath my desk, so I doodle on my notebook and pretend my mother's speaking in Greek. It's just a scene from a B horror movie, I tell myself. Soon, the credits will roll and it will all be over.

After school, my mother turns and smiles at me in the car. "I think that went pretty well. Your classmates seemed very interested."

I had told myself I was going to be controlled and mature. I was going to gently explain to my mother how she was devastating my life. But this is too much. My pulse begins to pound like I've just downed three Monster Energy drinks in under a minute.

"Why didn't you tell me?" I scream. "I can't believe you came to my class and you didn't tell me first!"

My mother looks wary. This isn't the mother-daughter moment she envisioned. "I wanted to surprise you, honey. I thought you'd like having me come talk about my business."

"Chickens, Mom?" I screech. "You really think I want you to come and talk to my friends about chickens and their *poop*?" I see her hurt look and I know I should shut up, but I'm so mad there's a supersonic buzzing in my head.

My mother's face grows carefully composed. This is her "I'm an adult, you're a hormonal preteen throwing a tantrum" look, which sets me off even more.

"Didn't you hear them laughing? They're all laughing at me, at our family. They think we're total weirdos!" My voice rises and breaks on the last word.

"They do not think we're weirdos," my mother crisply replies. "I simply told them about my new business. I'm sorry if this embarrassed you."

I know my mother planned this out as a fun surprise,

and I know I've hurt her feelings, but I just wish she would consider *my* feelings for once. She's so in love with her chickens that she hardly pays attention to anything else, including me. No, *especially* me. We don't speak for the rest of the car ride.

As soon as I walk in the door at home, my cell phone rings. "Wow," Alyssa says. "So that was interesting with your mom. You didn't know she was coming to class?"

"Are you kidding?" I feel a surge of gratitude that Alyssa called so quickly to sympathize. I actually feel tears prickle behind my eyelids, and I'm about do a major emotion dump when I hear a giggle, very soft, in the background. "Do you have me on speakerphone?" I ask suspiciously.

"No," Alyssa answers, but there's a false note in her voice.

"I gotta go." I hang up, feeling dizzy. Has there been a sudden shift in the space-time continuum? Am I suddenly living in an alternate universe where my best friend just pretended to be nice while actually laughing at me behind my back?

Paranoia is creeping into my bones, fogging my brain. I need to shake it off. I probably imagined the giggle. Suddenly I feel guilty that I suspect Alyssa of such a low deed. "Get a grip," I mutter to myself. I grab a ball and take Wilma outside. She immediately goes nuts, yapping and jumping into the air and running in circles—all over a dirty, grungy tennis ball. I wish my life could be so simple.

I throw the ball and she streaks across the yard, her little legs pumping so hard they're a blur. What Wilma lacks in size she makes up for in determination. She once came trotting up to me and proudly dropped a dead mouse at my feet. At first, I thought it was a piece of tree bark, but when I leaned down I saw the curled tail, the tiny ears. It looked so small and gray and...dead. I'm sure Wilma thought I was screaming with joy, because she sat down, cocked her head, and *grinned* at me.

"She's a terrier," my dad explained. "That's what terriers do; they catch vermin." He gave her a dog treat, but all I could think of was Stuart Little trying to zoom away from Wilma in his little red car. Sometimes life sucks that way. One minute you're minding your own business, tooling along in your sports car, and the next moment the jaws of fate are snapping at you, grinding you up for a snack. And of course, nobody knows until it's too late that they're about to become the next meal.

11

The next morning starts off nice, kind of like in *Titanic* when the orchestra's playing just before they hit the iceberg. (It took me forever to persuade my parents to let me watch that movie. My dad finally watched it with me and fast-forwarded through all the steamy parts.)

First, I decide to try a new hairstyle that Alyssa showed me last week. She's always after me to try something different with my hair, so I know she'll be pleased. Then, my mother makes chocolate chip pancakes, and she casually tells me that she went ahead and fed the chickens for me. I know she feels bad about our fight the day before. So do I, so I eat an extra pancake to show my appreciation. When I miss the bus because I took too long styling my hair, my mother doesn't get mad. She gives Derek and me a ride to school and tells me I get to pick the radio station, even though Derek insists it's his turn.

I make a quick pit stop at my locker and am hurrying down the hall when I hear a shriek behind me. I turn and there are Alyssa and Lydia walking together, with Emily and Sara tagging along. And Lydia's pointing at something on the floor behind me. "What *is* that?" She says it so loud that kids turn and stare. "It fell off your shoe!"

That's when the sinking feeling starts. It feels like the chocolate chips are turning into lead pellets in my stomach. I turn around and see what looks like a clod of dirt on the floor behind me.

"Just dirt," I announce, and try to kick it away. But Lydia and her entourage are already there, and it bounces off Lydia's foot.

She shrieks like it's a dead mouse and yells, "It's dried chicken poop! Dried chicken crap fell off your shoe!"

The lead pellets start churning in my stomach as I realize she's right. My mind flashes back to the day before, when I was throwing the ball for Wilma in the yard. The chickens must have planted some poop right where I was sure to step in it, knowing it would harden in the crevices of my sneaker overnight. And now everything's gone exactly according to their diabolical plan. I wouldn't even be surprised if the chickens had a long-range detonation device to make the clod fall at exactly the right moment. How else would it drop right when Lydia is behind me?

Now everybody's staring at this piece of crud and laughing as they kick it at each other. It breaks up into pieces, which causes more screams, and finally Blake Nash picks one up and flings it at Lydia. "Have some of Kate's crap!" he calls. Lydia deflects it with her books; she's laughing so hard she can't even shriek anymore.

Blake starts smelling his hands and making throw-up noises. "It reeks!" he shouts. "These crapkates reek!"

I guess he means like cupcakes, or crabcakes—I don't know, but everyone thinks it's really funny. They all start shouting, "Have a crapkate!" as they kick pieces at one another, and you have to wonder, are these kids really about to enter eighth grade next year?

And where are the teachers? Are they in on it, too, standing behind their doors, sniggering? Is the whole town in on it? Has it been named National Get Kate Walden Day without my knowing it? Which just shows my paranoia is in full swing, but can you blame me? It turns out the jaws of fate have picked me for their next cosmic snack. They've plucked me from my jazzy little red car and are crunching on my bones. Finally Mr. Greuschen sticks his head out of his classroom and yells for everyone to quiet down and get to class.

Through this whole sordid scene, Alyssa has been laughing while trying to look sympathetic and failing utterly. She shakes her head at me like, *Hey, it's just a little joke,* but a knot the size of Mount Rushmore is lodged in my throat.

I just stare at her like I don't know her. It turns out I don't, because Lydia grabs her by the arm and drags her away, and Alyssa doesn't even try to stay behind with me. She looks back and rolls her eyes like, *What can I do?* Even worse, I hear Lydia say, "I haven't laughed that hard since"—she pauses and glances at Alyssa—"since yesterday!"

And I know—*I know* for sure what I probably deep down knew all along, that I did hear a giggle on the phone yesterday, and that giggle was Lydia. Still, I can hardly believe it. Alyssa—my best friend of six years, my ding-dong ditch conspirator, my lemonade stand partner, the star of all my movies, who loves SpongeBob SquarePants and can eat half a can of Easy Cheese in one sitting just like me, who adores scary movies, and who told me all about her creepy uncle even though she's not supposed to tell anyone—my Alyssa, who braved the water tower, just abandoned me for Lydia.

Remember the snowball effect? Some pathetic cartoon character gets kicked into snow and starts rolling down a mountain. He turns into a humongous snowball and finally hits rock bottom and explodes. That's kind of how my day goes. Everywhere I go I hear *crapkate*! Even the *sixth graders* are saying it. I'm dreading lunch most of all, so when the bell rings I duck into the bathroom and stay there until it gets quiet. I consider sitting in a bathroom stall all period, but my stomach is rumbling so hard it hurts. Finally I can't stand it any longer. I head for the cafeteria and get a tray of food.

Even though I'm mad at Alyssa, I still look for her

because we *always* sit together and sitting alone is out of the question. A tiny part of me hopes that maybe, just maybe, there's a good reason why she ran off. Maybe she will apologize and explain everything, just like she did before.

Alyssa is sitting with Lydia and her friends. Mimi and Lizzy are there, too, chatting happily away, and there are *no empty seats*. No one saved me a seat. I'm so in shock I think my mouth actually drops open. This has *never* happened before. Most times, people won't even ask to sit in the seat next to Alyssa, because they know it's saved for me. And vice versa. But today she's rubbing shoulders with Lydia, laughing it up. I'm pretty sure she sees me out of the corner of her eye, but she ignores me.

It feels like everyone in the cafeteria is staring at me except Alyssa. Even Mimi and Lizzy shoot glances my way. The seats around them are full, but they don't try to make room for me.

For a moment, I'm afraid tears are actually going to spill all over my Tater Tots, which would be the final humiliation, not to mention making the taters inedible. My stomach is queasy and my face feels like there's steam rising off it.

Then a hand at a nearby table shoots up. Someone's waving at me, trying to get my attention. I focus on who it is, and my stomach sinks even lower. Margaret Yorkel. There's an empty space next to her. There's a bunch of empty spaces. The only one sitting with her is Doris Drayburn, who's half a step up from Margaret on the social ladder, mainly because Doris doesn't have bright red hair and freckles and crooked teeth.

Doris has the opposite problem. She has hair so mousy it's practically not even a color, and it matches her eyes. She has thick black glasses, and she always wears brown because that's her favorite color. Doris is practically a genius. I've heard she'll be studying high school level math and science next year. She's never gotten a B on her report card, except for gym class because she's really uncoordinated.

Doris is staring at me, munching on a Tater Tot with a sour look on her face, like she's eating a pickle instead of a fake potato. Of course, she always looks sour so it may not be because of me. If I sit with Margaret and Doris, my shaky social standing will plummet into the toilet. It will be like admitting, yes, this is my lot in life, this is where I belong, with the misfits and social outcasts. It's *so* not fair because I don't belong there at all. I've always had friends—but all of them are sitting with Lydia right now and ignoring me.

I only have a split second to decide—should I pretend I don't see Margaret and go to the nurse's office? I would have to put down my tray somewhere and everyone would watch as I walked alone out of the lunchroom. It would be too humiliating. I gaze around the crowded room, but panic has set in and I can't focus. Where's Kendall Carlton, who sits behind me in math class? We have fun joking around together. I could sit with her. Or what about Grace Devlin from Spanish? A blurred sea of faces stares back at me and no one else raises a hand to invite me over.

Then I think about Lydia standing up for Margaret the day before. No one expects the two of them to become best buddies because of that. If I eat lunch with Margaret and Doris, it just means I'm sitting with someone else for a day. Tomorrow, things will go back to normal. In the meantime, I can be nice to Margaret, who is trying very hard to get my attention. I can show my classmates that I'm not as petty as they are. In fact, sitting with Margaret will be a daring act of rebellion against the established social order.

I give Margaret a big smile, and then I sit down next to her, my head held high. I stuff a Tater Tot in my mouth, trying for casual. It tastes like salted plastic. Margaret leans close and stares into my face.

"Are you and Alyssa having a fight?" There's so much sympathy dripping from her words that I feel a fresh round of tears spring up. I close my eyes, try to swallow the Tater Tot, and gag. Margaret slaps me on the back and I finally choke it down. She peers over at Alyssa, trying to think of something nice to say. "It's kind of crowded around Alyssa, but that's just because you were late. I'm sure she wishes you were over there. You'll see, tomorrow will be different...." She trails off and takes a bite of her sandwich.

Even though that's exactly what I was thinking a moment ago, I shrug and poke my fork at another Tater Tot. I want to say, "Sure, I'll catch a seat over there tomorrow. No big deal." That's what I want to say, but the words stick in my throat. My eyes are burning, my heart is still pounding, and there's a sour, rejected feeling in the pit of my stomach. I open my mouth to agree with Margaret. Instead, resentment pours out.

"I'd much rather sit with you guys," I say, lying through my teeth. "I wouldn't sit with Alyssa if she were the only person in the cafeteria. I mean, look at her." I stab my fork in her direction. "Sucking up to Lydia, trying to be Miss Popular. I hate that kind of thing."

Doris glances over at me, probably surprised at the savagery in my voice.

"I'm not sitting with her tomorrow, or the day after, or any other day," I continue loudly. "Alyssa is a sucky friend."

Some girls at the next table glance over, and I know Alyssa will hear about my comment by the end of the day. Well, good, I think stubbornly. She deserves it. Margaret is watching me with a worried look, so I try to muster the energy to smile at her.

Doris gazes at me through her Coke-bottle glasses. "I don't think *sucky* is a word."

Have these girls not heard of contacts?

"It's probably considered slang," she goes on. "They do include colloquialisms in the dictionary, so it could officially be a word. I'm just not sure. It would be fun to look it up and see."

Fun? With a supreme effort, I manage not to roll my eyes.

"Yeah, that would be fun," Margaret agrees, but she doesn't sound too excited. Maybe there's hope for Margaret after all.

By the end of the day, sick despair is hardening into anger. Who does Alyssa think she is, dumping me like yesterday's flat soda and picking up some fruity, artificial new flavor of the day? We've spent the last two years saying how glad we were not to be one of Lydia's hangers-on, and now Alyssa's suddenly camping with the enemy. And she clawed her way next to Lydia at my expense. The enormity of the betrayal is almost too much to take in. I got braces, lost my best friend, and became a loser, all in one week.

When Alyssa marches over to my locker at the end of the day, she has the nerve to act like she's mad at *me*. She leans against a locker and gives me a cold stare.

"Jennifer Adams said you called me a sucky friend."

"Yeah, so?"

Alyssa has decided that the best defense is an over-the-top offense. She flicks back her long hair. "I can't believe you would say that."

Normally I would never carry on an argument in a school hallway where anyone can and will listen in, but I'm so mad I don't care.

"Stop acting all innocent," I snap. "You make fun of my family, you laugh at me behind my back, and you don't even save me a seat at lunch. You're so sucky, you don't even deserve to be called a friend."

"I was talking about your dog, not your family, and it was just for fun. Can't you take a joke? And you didn't show up for lunch. How am I supposed to know you're going to stroll in fifteen minutes late? You weren't there and then Lydia and Emily and Sara sat down. I can't believe you're acting like such a baby."

Sure enough, the entire hallway has gone quiet. Everyone, even the boys, are watching Kate Walden and Alyssa Jensen fight—hoping, no doubt, we'll start rolling on the floor, ripping each other's hair out. I find myself picturing it as if it were a scene in a movie. Close-ups of angry faces. Cutaway of me slamming shut my locker. Maybe a dolly shot down the hallway...

I refocus with an effort. It's not a movie. It's a fight with my best friend. "Baby?" I flare. "You are a pathetic wannabe. Trying to be Lydia's best buddy..."

"There's nothing wrong with having other friends," Alyssa cuts in coldly.

"Stop acting like you don't know what I'm talking about!" I practically scream at her.

I see something flicker in her face—is it anger, or guilt? She bites her lower lip. I should stop right there and let her make the next move. But once again I can't seem to shut up. Maybe I'm a little jealous. Of course Lydia wants to be friends with Alyssa. She has shiny blond hair and she's pretty and she looks like she should be in high school. Clearly Lydia doesn't want to be friends with me.

"Or maybe you really don't know what I'm talking about," I go on recklessly. "Maybe this is yet another blond moment for Duh-lyssa Jensen." I pretend to flick my hair away from my face and say in my best Alyssa voice: "Huh? Homework? I have long blond hair, so I don't need to be smart. Everyone loves dumb blondes, right?"

Alyssa's face turns red. She shakes her head but can't think of a thing to say. The girl desperately needs a script-writer. Finally she spits out, "You suck," and stomps away.

I grab my books and hurry outside, ignoring the stares. I feel like a zombie that's just been stabbed through the heart with a pair of scissors.

As soon as I get home that afternoon, I go straight to my room and throw myself on my bed. I stare at the ceiling, tears oozing from my eyelids and rolling onto the pillow. When I try to piece together what happened, exactly where things went wrong, I keep coming back to my mother and her chickens. If we lived in a regular house in town like normal people, Lydia wouldn't have seen a hen poop, Wilma wouldn't be rolling in the stuff, Derek wouldn't be shooting it from his slingshot, and it wouldn't be falling off my shoe at school. If we hadn't moved to this run-down farmette in the middle of nowhere, I would still be hanging out with Alyssa and other kids in the neighborhood. I would still have friends and a life.

Of course, I also wouldn't have a movie called *Night of the Zombie Chickens*. I shove this thought aside. I could have called it *Night of the Zombie Dogs* or *Night of the Zombie Hamsters*. Any animal would be easier to work with than our poltergeist poultry, with their beady eyes and evil hearts.

What kind of parent drags her kids away from all their friends? And why did my father agree to it? He could have put his foot down and said, "Let us think of the children." But no one said that; no one thought about me. I can hardly blame Alyssa for wanting a best friend who lives close by.

When I think of her, an even bigger knot wedges in my throat. Does she really like Lydia better than she likes me? It's such a silly question that I snort out loud. Lydia is popular and pretty. She's funny and does crazy things. When you're Lydia's friend, you're at the center of a whirlwind and there's never a dull moment. How can I compete with that? They've probably been hanging out together at the park for a while and Alyssa never told me. Maybe Lydia has been making fun of my movie behind my back.

Maybe everyone is laughing at me behind my back—poor, pathetic Crapkate, pretending to be a movie director. How lame is that? Why did I ever think I wanted to make movies, anyway?

I wish I had a magic crystal ball so I could figure out what everybody is really thinking. Lydia seemed excited about being in my movie, but then she treated the shoot like a big joke. Alyssa said she was sorry about the way she acted, but then she kept acting that way. And I wanted to make up with Alyssa, but instead I screamed mean things at her.

The world suddenly seems murky, like someone's taken all the nice, crisp lines of a picture and smudged them. Things have never been so twisted up and confusing. A chill creeps inside me as I wonder if this is only the beginning. Is this what growing up is really like, where things get so complicated that you don't know who you are anymore? Maybe all the TV shows and magazines are lying—maybe it's not so cool to be an adult after all.

By the time my mother calls me for dinner, my head is throbbing and so are my teeth. I tell her I'm not hungry and that I don't feel well, but she insists I come down and sit with them anyway. Of course, when one of her hens gets sick, she babies it like it's a newborn infant. I drag myself into my chair at the dinner table and gaze at my plate. Baked chicken. I shove it away. The last thing I want to eat is a dead chicken.

"What's the matter?" my dad asks. "Not hungry?"

I shake my head.

"If she doesn't eat, she doesn't get dessert," Derek pipes up. "Right, mom? That means I can have her cookies."

"You're such a baby," I mumble. The thought of him getting my dessert does make me reconsider the chicken. I stab it with my fork. This actually feels kind of good, so I stab it again.

"Bad day?" my mom asks.

I nod. Stab.

"You're not supposed to play with your food, Dumbo," Derek says. "Right, mom?"

"Enough, Derek," my father warns.

"She's playing with her food. That means no dessert," Derek whines.

"Yes, I had a bad day," I say loudly. "And no, you can't have my dessert. I'll give it to Wilma before you get a crumb."

Wilma perks up at her name and shoves her snout in my lap. I slip her a piece of chicken.

"Chocolate chips are bad for dogs," Derek fires back.

"Wilma has a cast-iron stomach. She can eat anything."

"Mom! She's going to make Wilma sick."

All this for a couple of chocolate chip cookies. My parents look at each other across the table, no doubt wishing they had decided to raise gerbils instead of children. Can whiny kids drive parents to divorce?

"Shut up, Derek!" I bark.

"Kate, that's enough. Derek, one more word and Wilma will be eating your dessert, too." My mother looks frazzled. My dad rubs his eyes. He looks tired as he turns to me.

"Kate, tell us what happened."

I shake my head. The last thing I want to do is talk about my day over dinner. "It's nothing," I mutter.

"Something must have happened," my dad says. "You look terrible."

"Thanks, Dad."

"She always looks terrible," Derek pipes up.

My dad points a fork at him. "That's cookie number one, buddy. You want to go for two?"

Derek gets a hangdog look and shakes his head.

"I don't want to talk about it," I say. "Just forget about it."

My parents exchange another look. Then my mother actually mouths the word *hormones* at my dad.

"Can you not do that, please?" I say loudly. "I'm sitting right here."

My mother sighs. We all pick at our food. I think about Lydia and her parents. They probably used to all sit down together at dinner, just like we do. Lydia and her sister probably thought everything was fine, and all that time their father had a girlfriend on the side.

I stare at my dad. Suddenly it feels like I don't know him at all. He spends most of his day at work with strangers. It's like he has a whole life apart from us. He has secrets we don't know about. And complications. Could he really decide to leave us behind one day, like Lydia's dad? How could anyone be so important to him that he would abandon his family?

My dad is frowning at his chicken. I wish again that I had a crystal ball so I could find out what he's thinking. It doesn't seem fair that my life is falling apart *and* I have to worry about my parents.

"Well," my mother finally says, "if it makes you feel any better, I had a bad day, too."

I'm not sure why this is supposed to make me feel better. I've completely lost my appetite, but I eye the chicken anyway, trying to figure out how little I can eat and still get dessert.

"What happened?" my dad asks.

My mother slathers butter on a piece of bread. "One of my hens has a prolapsed vent."

"That sounds bad," Derek says in a superconcerned voice. "What does that mean?" It's completely obvious that he's trying to suck up and get his cookie back, but of course my parents don't realize it.

My mother nods. "It is bad. A prolapsed vent is when the lower part of the oviduct turns inside out and comes out through the vent."

Derek and I stare at each other. I know better than to ask, but he's trying to win points.

"The what comes through the what?"

My mother smiles at him. "The oviduct is like the fallopian tube. So the egg travels down the tube and the vent is where the egg comes out. Sometimes, hens lay an egg that's too big and it makes their oviduct come out and you have to push it back in. Hemorrhoid cream is supposed to help; isn't that funny?" My mother says all this matter-of-factly. She takes a bite of her chicken. "The problem is, the vent got bloody and then the other hens started to peck at it."

I'm so revolted I can only stare at her, but Derek screws up his face and shouts, "Gross!"

"I know," my mother says, warming to her topic. "I had to separate the hen from the others. I read that they'll keep pecking at her vent, and they can even pull out her intestines—"

"Do we have to talk about this at dinner!" I shout. Even my dad's face looks green. He's probably just as sick of chickens as I am. Maybe that's why he spends so much time behind closed doors talking on the phone. "This is not what normal families talk about! It's disgusting!"

My mother puts down her fork. "You do not have to shout, Kate."

All the horrible feelings from the day swell inside me until I need to either scream or burst into tears again. So I keep screaming. "Yes I do! It's the only way you hear anything! I don't want to hear about the chickens' bloody intestines, or their parasites or their worms!" I shove myself back from the table. "All we ever hear about anymore are your stupid hens! They're all you think about! I'm sick of them! They've ruined my life and so have you, and you don't even care!"

I can feel more tears coming, so I jump up and run for the door. I catch a glimpse of my mother's face. She looks stunned.

"Kate!" my dad calls.

"You should have said no!" I scream at him. He looks confused, but by then I'm already out of the room and up the stairs.

I slam shut my door. "I hate everything!" I shout.

I'm still in shock, but I'm not sure if it's because of the gruesome hen story or the fact that I just screamed at my mother. What has happened to me? A couple of years ago, I wouldn't have dreamed of yelling at her. My mom and I were buddies. That was when she paid attention to me.

Is this what happens when kids grow up? Do parents lose interest? Sometimes I wish my mother would still do things like push the hair out of my face and say, "Anybody in there?" I used to complain whenever she did it, so that's probably why she stopped. Still, she should know better than to listen to every little thing I say.

Sometimes I even wish she would get out our goofy-looking ostrich. We named him Ollie. Ollie has a superlong neck covered with penciled lines from measuring Derek and me ever since we were toddlers. My mother always exclaimed at how much I'd grown, even if it was only a sliver. She hasn't pulled out Ollie once since we moved to the farmhouse.

Of course, the reason is that I'm way too old for that. I'm a seventh grader—why would I want to be measured like a little girl? I'll be in high school in two years. I'm practically an adult. Sometimes I wish I could be a clueless fourth grader again. Those were the good old days.

I stare at my reflection in the mirror. My dad is right, I look terrible. I look like a sixth grader. And if there's a problem in my parents' marriage, I probably just made it worse.

"Good going," I whisper to myself. "Now she really hates you. She'll probably adopt a hen to be her new daughter."

My reflection nods in agreement.

13

As soon as he sees me the next morning, Blake Nash bawls, "Crap alert! Crap alert!" and everybody starts laughing.

"Hey, Braceface, what's on the bottom of your shoe?" Paul Corbett calls.

"You, if you don't shut up," I mutter.

"Look at me!" Blake shouts. "I'm a famous movie director! I'm making a movie about chickens!"

Paul runs around, squawking and flapping his arms. Blake chases after him, acting like he's shooting with a camera. Then he stares down at his shoes and pretends to gag. "I'm full of crap!"

"No, your movie is crap," Paul jokes.

I stalk past them toward my locker, but I can feel my

face burning. I can't believe they're laughing at my movie. Three days ago I thought people would be begging to be in it. Now it's joke material.

None of this would have happened if I hadn't invited Lydia to be a zombie. And that, of course, was Alyssa's idea.

Lydia sails by, surrounded by her wannabes. Alyssa's in the thick of them. She gives me the cold shoulder, then leans in close to Lydia, whispering. Lydia glances my way and grins. I cringe inside. I wish I could ask Alyssa what's happened to her. Instead, I pretend like I haven't noticed either of them.

"Crapkate! How's it going?" Lydia calls over carelessly, like Crapkate has been my nickname forever and there's nothing wrong with it—like it's Spike or Mags or La-La, which are all fun nicknames of people I know. This bothers me most of all, this pretending like it's totally okay to call me that—like I should just accept such a lame name.

"That's not my nickname," I say in a loud voice, but they've already moved on. A few sixth graders stare at me. There's nothing like having people watch you talk to thin air to make you feel stupid. I slam my locker shut and stalk to my first class.

All day long, people joke about crap and I tell them to shut up. Then they act like I'm a sour head who can't take a little fun. And maybe I am, but the more I hear it, the more it grates on my nerves. Crap might be funny, but not when your name is attached to it. Secretly I'm hoping Alyssa might still apologize, but she's always busy in the center of a throng of girls. Okay, maybe making fun of her hair and calling her Duh-lyssa were out of line. Still, *I'm* not the one who should be apologizing. Not first, anyway.

Apparently Alyssa has decided I don't exist anymore. At lunch, the seats around her are full again, even though I hurry as fast as I can to the lunchroom.

That's when it really, finally hits me. I've been cast out. I *do* belong with Margaret and Doris now. I've become Crapkate Walden, purveyor of chicken poop, daughter of a deranged female farmer in the throes of a midlife crisis, sister of the village idiot, friend to no one.

My shoulders sag in defeat as I sit next to Margaret and Doris. Margaret gives me a big smile, which makes me feel even worse. I've spent a lot of years avoiding Margaret. Surely she picked up on that. Yet now, when she could snub me as payback, Margaret has offered me a seat at the lunch table. I'm such a mess of mixed-up feelings that I half wish Margaret *would* ignore me. I'm pretty sure I deserve it.

"Did you hear about the *Annie* auditions, Kate?" Margaret asks me. "They're in a couple of weeks. Are you trying out?"

I shake my head. "What about you?"

"I don't know. I might." Margaret wipes the lid of her soda can before opening it. She takes a bite of her sandwich, then dabs her fingers with her napkin. Margaret, it turns out, is a neat freak.

"How about you, Doris?" I ask. "Are you going to try out?"

Doris has a milk mustache. I offer her a napkin, but she just looks blankly at it and crumples it up. With all her supercharged brain cells, you'd think Doris would get the concept of personal grooming. Maybe all geniuses are slobs. Out of the blue, she starts to croak: *Tomorrow! Tomorrow! I love you, tomorrow. . . .*"

All the tables around us turn and stare. I catch Alyssa and Lydia exchanging a look like, *Can you believe she just did that?*

"Doris!" I hiss. "What are you doing?"

She shrugs. "Just demonstrating why I'm not trying out. I'm completely tone-deaf."

"You could have just told me," I mutter.

"Anyway," she says, "I don't look like Annie."

Margaret shakes her head. "It doesn't matter. Mr. Cantrell ordered a wig from New York, and it just arrived this morning. You should see it, Kate. It's so cute. He's got it in the music classroom. Whoever plays Annie gets to wear the wig."

The entire female seventh- and eighth-grade population is already buzzing about the red wig. I must hear the word *cute* at least fifty times after lunch. In fact, it quickly gets dubbed the Cute Red Wig. I take a detour on my way to Business Ed and walk past the music classroom, hoping to catch a glimpse of it. There it is, a curly red mop sitting on a black plastic head. It is, I have to admit, very cute. Even I feel a moment of weakness at the thought of standing onstage in the Cute Red Wig, belting out "Tomorrow" to an adoring crowd. If I got the part, it would definitely improve my dismal social standing. The whole singing requirement seems like such an inconvenient detail.

The sign-up sheet is already filling up. I notice Lydia's name in her big, flowing script, and Alyssa's name just below it, followed by her signature happy face. Staring at her little squiggle, so cheerful and sickening, reminds me that I've not only lost my best friend, I've lost the star of my movie. I couldn't come up with an ending when Alyssa and I were buddies. How will I ever write the perfect ending now?

What's even worse, I'm not sure I care. A part of me feels like calling it quits and selling my camera. No other kid I know dreams about being a Hollywood director, which just goes to show the whole idea must be pretty lame. *Lamekate* could be my new nickname, right up there with *Crapkate*.

I always thought *heartache* was just a mushy word, but my heart really does hurt as I stare at Alyssa's name. I feel like I've fallen into a deep, dark pit. My chest burns and my throat feels tight as I grab the pen and cross out her happy face until it's a black gob of ink. I'm tempted to gouge out her name, but it doesn't feel like nearly enough. Alyssa turned her back on me and abandoned me to turn into a social zombie. I want her to know what it's like to roam the hallways like one of the living dead. I want her to know what heartache feels like.

I need a plan.

The thought makes me feel a tiny bit better. The pit feels a little less deep, a little less dark. I suddenly have a goal. I will teach Alyssa a lesson.

The rest of the day passes by in a blur. Suddenly I'm fair game for Blake Nash and Paul Corbett. They act like I smell like chicken poop and they make fun of my movie. Lizzy and Mimi shoot guilty looks at me, but no one says a word. It's like I've become invisible. If I walk directly up to them, they say hi and act nice, but they quickly find a reason to leave, or they talk to each other like they've forgotten I'm there. No one stands up for me. I wonder if this is how Margaret feels all the time.

I always thought that Margaret was a pushover, letting the boys make fun of her. Now I see it's not so simple. I've been excluded. I'm alone, and that makes me an easy target, just like Margaret. I guess that's why girls always go everywhere in a pack. There's strength in numbers.

It reminds me of Henrietta, one of my mother's hens. She's at the very bottom of the social pecking order, kind of like me. You can spot Henrietta right away. She always looks nervous and ready to bolt. When she sidles up to the feeders, the other hens chase her away until they're finished eating. In the yard, she's usually off by herself, pecking at bugs and looking forlorn. She has bald spots on her back where the other hens have gone after her.

It seems like hens and humans have a lot in common, except on humans the scars don't show. I always used to wonder if Henrietta felt sad. Was she lonely?

"Can't we do something for her?" I asked my mother once. "How can we get the other hens to leave her alone?"

My mother shook her head. "I know it seems mean, but that's the chicken world. It's how they're wired. Anything we do would probably just make things worse for her."

The truth is, there's only one way Henrietta can improve her lot in life. She has to prove she's tougher than at least one of the other hens. If she can out-scratch and out-peck someone in the flock, she won't be at the bottom of the heap anymore. Poor Henrietta can't do it, though; she's just too timid and scatterbrained.

Well, I'm not Henrietta. I have to fight back. It feels like I have a huge bald spot on my back where Alyssa dug in her claws. In my classes, I daydream about how I can rip her from Lydia's side. It seems I've turned into a mental zombie, too, because I can't think of a single good idea.

In the meantime, I sit with Margaret and Doris again at lunch, and I finally learn what social outcasts talk about among themselves—other kids in class, homework, teachers, movies, music. Pretty much all the same stuff that popular kids talk about. And I learn a few things about them.

Doris has two fish. Margaret has a cat named Tabitha. Also, Margaret is an avid reader of teen romances. This is more shocking than learning she listens to Eminem. Margaret dreams about romance? It's like trying to imagine my parents being romantic—I have to quickly shove the thought out of my mind.

The truth is, it's hard to focus on what Margaret and Doris are saying. I smile and nod, but it's like I hear them through water. Out of the corner of my eye I'm always watching Alyssa, listening for her voice, wondering what she's thinking. Wondering why she's acting this way. With every day that passes, our friendship fades a little further into the murky gloom called Ancient History.

A thought nags at me as I pretend not to watch her. Maybe she has secretly wanted to be Lydia's friend ever since Lydia showed up in fifth grade. Maybe Alyssa was only hanging out with me until she got Lydia's attention. I stare at the back of her head in the lunchroom. She must feel my eyes burning into her because she suddenly glances around. Good. Let her be nervous. Very nervous. There's a zombie out to get her, and it's hungry for blood.

I think about it during dinner as I play with my food. I think about it when I'm supposed to be doing my homework. It keeps me awake at night. I need a plan. Finally, I decide the only way to solve the problem is to hold an epic brainstorming session.

In the past, Alyssa and I always brainstormed together, preferably at her house because she had better supplies. Her mother always kept plenty of Fritos, Doritos, and Cheetos on hand, and lots of soda. At my house, we had to eat Garden Veggie Straws and drink seltzer. My mother always says we are what we eat and she doesn't want an artificially flavored daughter.

At Alyssa's, we'd stay up late and hole up in her room. After we fed our creative brain cells, we'd start calling out ideas. One of us would write them all down, no matter how stupid. Usually, we ended up laughing hysterically, hopped up on sugar and junk food. We always came up with a lot of dumb ideas, but usually there were good ones, too.

Still, I'm sure I can brainstorm just fine on my own. I sneak downstairs and check the fridge. There's organic milk, orange juice, and two cans of O'Leary's Natural Pomegranate soda. I sigh and scoop up the cans. In the back of the refrigerator, I find a half-empty can of Easy Cheese that Alyssa smuggled in on her last sleepover. I grab that, along with a jar of whole pickles. I scrounge around until I find the other two must-haves—a big pad of blank white paper and colored markers that squeak when I write with them. I like the squeaking. Whatever I'm writing immediately sounds more creative.

It's getting late by this time, but that's okay. Another rule is that brainstorming must take place late at night. My parents are already in bed and the house is spookily quiet. It's perfect. I arrange all the supplies around me on my bed. Then I fish a pickle out of the jar, spray Easy Cheese on it, and take a big bite. I'm convinced that pickles unleash the imagination. There's something about crunching down on that cold, green, vinegary, cheesy deliciousness that makes the mouth and the brain salivate. I polish off my first pickle and down a soda. So far, so good. It's not quite the same without someone to laugh with, though. Laughter definitely helps crack open the creative sinus passages.

I once read about how, in India, they have laugh clubs, where people get together just to laugh. They take it really seriously and even do laughing exercises. I try an experimental chuckle. It's kind of fun, so I try a deep "ha-ha-ha." It feels so bizarre to be giggling alone, at nothing, that it makes me laugh for real, and I have to stick my head under my pillow so I don't wake up my parents.

I uncap a purple marker and grab my pad. The smell of sugary grape Kool-Aid fills the room. My mother is still buying me fruit-scented colored markers. I guess she hasn't noticed that I'm not ten years old anymore. Too busy with her chickens to pay attention. I stare at the ceiling, the marker quivering over the bare paper.

"Boil her in corn oil."

Hmmm, that seems a little extreme. I write it down anyway.

"Shave off her hair while she's sleeping." *Squeak, squeak.*

"Slip something in her food that will make her smell like BO." I kind of like this one so I put a star next to it.

"Drench her in hamburger juice and unleash a pack of hounds."

Okay, I stole that last one from the movie *Cheaper by the Dozen*. Still, all the ideas seem kind of flat, maybe because there's no one to laugh at them.

I sigh and grab a red marker. While I'm brainstorming, I might as well work on the ending to my movie, too. There has to be a way to finish it without Alyssa. The marker smells like rotting strawberries, which doesn't sit well with the pickle in my belly. I hold the marker away from my nose and try to think.

"Buy a life-size doll with a long blond wig. Put it in bed under the covers. A zombie attacks it."

Even my voice sounds flat. I try to inject some enthusiasm. "LOTS of blood ALL OVER. The END."

Hmmm, maybe something with more action.

"Derek in blond wig and dress runs into woods. Dad-zombie chases. Branches start SHAKING. Add GROWLING, CRUNCHING bone sounds. BLOOD spatters the lens. The END."

The marker squeaks as I write this down. Nothing else comes to mind. I fish out another pickle, squirt twice the amount of Easy Cheese on it, and gobble it down. A second later, I belch up cheesy vinegar. If Alyssa were here it would be funny, but right now it's just nasty. I fan the air and read over what I wrote.

They aren't the happy ending I'd hoped for. To have a happy ending, I need Mallory smiling, and that's impossible without Alyssa.

The pickles are starting to percolate in my stomach. Another whiff of sickening strawberry doesn't help. I lie back in bed. My two problems start running together in my mind. Too bad I can't just turn Alyssa into a crazed zombie. That would make her unpopular at school. I could slip zombie pills into her lunch. I could film her as she chases down our classmates and gnaws on them with her blackened teeth. . . .

When I wake up, my alarm feels like a jackhammer drilling a hole in my head. My stomach rumbles queasily. Did I really eat two jumbo pickles and half a can of Easy Cheese last night? I read hopefully through my list of ideas, but there's not a decent one in the bunch. So much for brainstorming.

At school, I feel like I'm sleepwalking through the hallways. Alyssa passes by in a whirl of girls, all trying to laugh the loudest. They stare sideways at me as they pass, and I wish I could be like Violet in *The Incredibles* and make myself disappear. It's hopeless. Alyssa's in with the in crowd and nothing's going to dislodge her.

At least it's Friday. I slump into a seat in choir, feeling defeated. I've expended my best efforts and all I have to show for it is a sour stomach. I have no plan for Alyssa, and no ending for my movie.

I glance up when Mr. Cantrell plays a riff from "Tomorrow," the song from *Annie*. Lydia is telling him that he should make her Annie.

"No, really," she insists. "Can't you just see me as Annie all dolled up in a red wig? It'll be hilarious." She pretends to stomp onstage and strikes a pose. *"Tomorrow, tomorrow, I love you tomorrow,"* she shrieks at the top of her voice, and everyone laughs. Even pale, serious Mr. Cantrell smiles. "And I can dance, too." Lydia does a slapstick tap dance.

Then, Alyssa and her other pals get up and do a crazy dance with her. It makes my stomach turn, but Mr. Cantrell laughs. I can see he thinks Lydia would make a great Annie because of her energy. With her luck, Lydia will get the part *and* the Cute Red Wig. Everyone wants to wear it. In my weaker moments, even I do.

That's when it hits me. Everyone wants to wear it. An idea explodes in my brain with the mega-voltage of a nuclear warhead. I know exactly how to teach Alyssa a lesson. A cold prickle slides down my spine, but I'm not sure if it's fear or excitement. Maybe both.

Sometimes, flashes of genius hit when you least expect them. I sit for a moment in class, but no one seems to have noticed my gasp of excitement. That's because no one pays any attention to me. First, I savor my idea. It's so easy, yet so impossible. . . .

Then, I immediately tell Mr. Cantrell that I feel sick, which is kind of true after watching Lydia's and Alyssa's silly dance. He excuses me to go see the nurse, and half an hour later, my mother pulls up to the curb.

At home, I dash into my room, lock the door, and run to my computer. If my life were a movie, then Alyssa would be the villain. Everyone knows the villain doesn't win. The good guy always comes out on top. That means I need to write an ending where I triumph and Alyssa gets her just reward.

It reminds me of a movie my dad made me watch once called *The Maltese Falcon*. I wasn't too excited, because it's old and in black and white, and the lead actor's name is Humphrey Bogart. Not too promising. But my dad said his nickname was Bogie, which is kind of cool. He said if I wanted to be a Hollywood director I had to see this movie because it's one of the best-ever examples of *film noir*.

So I looked up *film noir* (pronounced "nwar") on the Internet. It's a film style that was really popular back in the nineteen forties and fifties. The movies are mostly crime dramas with harsh lighting, deep shadows, and plenty of hard-boiled characters. Most of the endings are not happy. Some of the acting is kind of corny, but now it's one of my favorite movie genres.

In *The Maltese Falcon*, Bogie plays this tough detective who falls for a Beautiful Dame. It turns out she's setting him up to take the fall for a murder she committed. Bogie's too clever, though. He outsmarts her and sends her to prison, even though she's probably the love of his life. Like I said, not a lot of happy endings.

So here's my genius idea. I'll write a scene like something out of *The Maltese Falcon*. I'll be Bogie, who makes sure the Beautiful Dame gets what she deserves.

It's not like I want to get Alyssa expelled or anything. I just want her to know how it feels to get dumped by people you think are your friends.

There's this old saying my mom loves to quote about not

judging people until you've walked a mile in their shoes. I guess that's because you don't really understand what someone else is going through until you go through it yourself. That's why I think it will do Alyssa good to tromp around in my size sixes for a while. They may pinch since she's a size seven, but as my dad loves to say, no pain, no gain. So really, I'm doing Alyssa a favor. I'm helping her to understand other people's pain.

Once my computer's up and running, I open my script-writing software and gaze at the blank screen. The first words are always the hardest. I glance around my room, searching for inspiration. A photo on my bulletin board catches my eye. It's Alyssa and me when we were seven, laughing like crazy at something, our heads thrown together. There's another photo of us on my tenth birthday, holding up a pink cake, blowing out the candles together.

I push back from my desk and wander over to the open window. It feels like it should be a cold, drizzly day, but the sky gleams deep blue, like someone cranked up the color knob on the TV. As I close my eyes and the sun pours through the glass, warming my face, it occurs to me that maybe I'm overreacting. After all, friends have fights all the time. Friends go their separate ways.

A breeze stirs the trees outside and I can hear their leaves whispering. I've always loved trees. They weather storms, wind, hail. They stand their ground. They lean on each other, they protect each other. Alyssa and I were like two intertwined trees. Other people had fights, but not us. We always had each other's back. We were closer than sisters. She was like my second half, my cosmic twin.

I guess that's why I've never been hurt this much by anyone in my entire life. I've never been so mad, either, which makes me feel like Dr. Jekyll and Mr. Hyde. There's no point in denying it. I miss Alyssa. I wish I could call her and pretend like nothing happened. I wish we could shoot the perfect last scene for *Night of the Zombie Chickens*.

I could call her. But what if I say sorry and then she doesn't? What if she pretends it was all my fault or, even worse, acts like she doesn't care if I'm sorry or not?

A shadow falls over me and I open my eyes. A cloud has slid across the sun. I push away from the window, feeling chilled.

If I did call, Alyssa would probably be with Lydia. She would pretend to be nice and then laugh at me behind my back. After all, she's best buddies with the MPG while I've come down with a bad case of Crapkateitis.

I grit my teeth and sit back down at my desk. I can't call Alyssa. What I can do is come up with a plan. If I have a plan, that means I'm doing something. I'm not just giving up like Henrietta. And once I have a plan, I'm pretty sure I'll feel better.

I crack my knuckles and stare at the blank screen. I stare

at the blinking cursor. I stare out the window. Hey, even J. K. Rowling probably gets writer's block.

Finally, the words start to flow:

INT: SCHOOL HALLWAY—DAY

BOGIE strolls down the hall with
MARGARET YORKEL.

                    BOGIE
        Oh, look, what's that?

Bogie points to a piece of paper.
Margaret picks it up and opens it.

                    MARGARET
                (reading aloud)
        "Alyssa, please meet me after
        fifth period in the music room.
        I need to ask you something.
        Jake."

(This is where knowing Alyssa so well comes in handy. NOBODY else knows she has a crush on Jake. She says she's over it, but I know she will be in that music room, no matter what.)

                    BOGIE
    I wonder if Alyssa dropped it.

                    MARGARET
    Should we give it back to her?

                    BOGIE
    I can't. I'm not talking to her.
    Why don't you give it to her?
    I'm sure she'll appreciate it.

CUT TO:

Gym class. Margaret approaches
Alyssa and hands her the note. Alyssa
opens it and her face goes dead
white.

I write the rest of the afternoon until the script is done.
I consider teaching Lydia a lesson, too, but it seems silly.
It would be like getting mad at the sun for burning you—
what's the point? Strange as it sounds, I know Lydia doesn't
have anything against me. She must know that she ruined
my friendship with Alyssa, but she's probably too busy being
popular to worry about how I feel. If someone told her I
was miserable, she might put an arm around my shoulders

and say "Why so serious?" in her best Joker imitation, but that would be it. The stories about the chickens, kicking the poop around—it's all just laughs to her. It's about creating a whirlwind of energy and being at the center of it. Lydia is just being herself. Alyssa is being her anti-self.

So my script focuses on Alyssa. And everyone has their part to play, even Mr. Cantrell. The timing is important. It needs to happen before the *Annie* auditions. In fact, the sooner, the better. I study the calendar and circle Monday in red crayon on my calendar. D-Day (Duh-lyssa Day) is three days away.

Over the weekend, I make preparations. I slave over the note from Jake. I have no idea what his handwriting looks like, but I'm pretty sure Alyssa doesn't, either. When I try for masculine, it looks like Superman wrote it. When I tone it down, it's like something my mother would pen. How do boys write? Sloppily, I decide. I finally craft something I think will work. I notice my mother watching me as I gather a few more props around the house.

Both my parents have been eyeing me a lot since my outburst at the dinner table. My mother never said another word, and I figured she had forgotten about it. I should have known better. On Sunday night, my dad and Derek disappear right after dinner, and that's when I know I'm in for it. My mother clears her throat and says she wants to talk to me. We sit down at the kitchen table. My mother looks very formal and serious. She clears her throat again.

"Kate, you said a lot of things last week, and I've been thinking about them. You said that you felt I was ruining your life. I suppose you mean the talk I gave in your class?"

That already seems like it happened another lifetime ago. I could tell her it's just the tip of the iceberg. Instead, I gaze at my gnawed fingernails. "That, and other things."

My mother nods, as if now we're getting somewhere. "What other things?"

I shrug. How can I explain everything that's going on in my life? She wouldn't understand.

"You mentioned the hens," my mother goes on. "You think they're somehow to blame?"

I stare at the tiny cracks in our old wooden table. I never noticed them before. I can feel my mother waiting. Why is it suddenly so hard to talk to her? She's expecting me to say something. I take a deep breath.

"If you hadn't gotten the chickens, then we wouldn't have moved out here. I would still be living in town near all my friends." I feel a spurt of anger just talking about it. "I would still *have* some friends."

"You have lots of friends," my mother protests. "Alyssa and Lizzy and Mimi…"

It feels like a hot needle pricks me each time she says a name.

"Has anybody invited me over lately? Do I go anywhere?" I let this sink in. "You're just too busy with your chickens to notice. Everybody at school makes fun of me. You know what my nickname is now? Crapkate. As in chicken crap, mom! CHICKEN CRAP!"

My volume level has switched to "high." I can't seem to dial it down even though I know my mother's trying to help. She *can't* help, though, so it just makes it worse.

"They think it's weird we have chickens. They think my movie is stupid. And you know what? They're right!"

My mother looks worried, like she's not sure how to handle this. "Now, Kate," she says, "it's normal to have fights with your friends. I'm sure it will all blow over soon."

She always used to know the right thing to say. Deep down, I was hoping she might still save the day. It's clear she can't, though. I'm on my own.

"Is there . . . anything else bothering you?" she asks.

Like that's not enough. I shake my head. But then, out of nowhere, I blurt, "Do you think Dad is having an affair?"

I don't know who is more stunned, her or me. I can't believe I just said it out loud.

My mother laughs. "Of course not!" She gets a funny look on her face, then adds more slowly, "Why do you ask that?"

I've gnawed all my fingernails down to nubs, so I chew on a piece of hair. "Nothing. No reason."

"Kate, you must have had a reason for asking that."

"No," I say quickly. "I was just...it doesn't matter. It was a stupid question."

I can tell the idea hasn't occurred to my mother before this second. I want to kick myself for putting the thought in her head. Now she's gazing suspiciously at me.

"Have you heard something, or seen something?"

She's starting to look a little unhinged. I need to fix the mess I'm making, quick. "It's just...Lydia Merritt's parents got divorced last summer. He was having an affair. So it's been on my mind, that's all. It was a dumb question. Dad would never do that."

My mother nods. "Of course your dad would never do that. You should know that." But I can tell I haven't stopped the gears from turning in her head. Is she remembering all the nights he's been working late? The private phone calls?

With an effort, she pulls herself together. "Now, about your friends..."

I stand up. "Don't worry, Mom. It'll all work out."

She nods, dazed. "Yes, it will. You'll see."

I walk away and she doesn't call me back. I guess there's nothing left to say.

That night, I carefully stash everything in my backpack. I'm ready. Lying in bed, I go over my script again, looking for problems. Actually, there are plenty. I try not to think about how wrong things could go. One thing I know for sure—my parents won't be very understanding if I'm expelled from school.

I can hear them arguing in their room as I try to get to sleep, but I can't tell what it's about. Their voices rise and fall. My mother sounds upset. What have I done? I bury my head under my pillow. When I finally fall asleep, their harsh whispers seem to follow me, swirling like dark shadows in my dreams.

17

Monday dawns crisp and clear. I know because I'm awake, watching the sun rise outside my window. A strange anxiety fills me, as if I have a big final exam in front of me, or a huge audition. I have to make a decision. I can get up and be Crapkate for another day, or I can do something about it.

Or I can tell my mother I'm sick and stay in bed under the covers all day. I do feel ill as I swing my legs over the side of the bed and sit up. My stomach feels tight and nervous and I know why.

I can't do it.

My plan suddenly seems silly, and dangerous. It's one thing to write it down on paper. I must have been crazy to think I would actually pull it off. The idea of ditching the plan fills me with relief. I'll file the script away with all my other half-baked ideas. No one ever needs to know.

Still, it's hard when I arrive at school. The hallways fill with students, but no one calls out my name. People's eyes slide past me, pretending they don't see me. I spot Alyssa and for a moment her eyes flicker toward me. Then she turns her back and laughs loudly at a comment from Lydia. They're standing in front of the *Annie* sign-up sheet. Lydia writes something as they snort and giggle together. I duck my head and act like I don't notice.

After they leave, I wander over to see what they were up to. I thought maybe they removed their names, but they're still there. Margaret finally signed up, I notice. That's when I see it. Someone drew a cartoon face by her name that's so covered in dots it looks like she's got the chicken pox. The glasses are huge circles and the hair looks like electrified snakes.

A bolt of anger sizzles through me. Alyssa has gone too far. Now she's making fun of poor Margaret. She and Lydia should pick on someone who can fight back. I take out a pen and scribble in the face until it's an inky blue blob. As I turn away, I know what needs to be done.

"It's on," I mutter. Luckily, the props for my script are still in my backpack. I grab the fake note from Jake Knowles and stick it in my pocket. Panic seizes me as I search the crowded hallway. I need to find Margaret and plant the fake note, but she's nowhere to be seen. Did she go to class early? Could she have picked this of all days to stay home sick?

"Hi, Kate!" Margaret's voice is so close behind me it makes me jump.

"Margaret, there you are!"

She eyes me curiously. "Were you looking for me?"

"No," I say quickly. "I just thought—do you want to walk to class?"

She shrugs. "Sure. I just have to grab something out of my locker first."

We head for her locker and she twirls the combination. I nervously glance at my cell phone to check the time.

Margaret's locker is as neat as a pin. I feel a little sad as I gaze at her carefully hung sweater, her color-coded paper organizer, and the accessories lined up with military precision—a comb, a hairbrush, a lip gloss, even a lint brush. Maybe this is Margaret's way of feeling in control of her life. Maybe being superneat makes it easier to deal with the insults and the chaos that swirl around her every day.

"Hey, Margarine, who barfed on your face?" Paul Corbett slams shut his locker and saunters over.

Margaret carefully nudges a stray paper back into place. She keeps her head down, but I can see her cheeks turning red. Before, I might have been too afraid to say anything, but now I've got nothing to lose.

"Hey, Paulie, who supersized your nose?" I shoot back.

Paul got hit in the nose during a fight last year and ever since then it's looked kind of lumpy. "What's the matter, did the doctor use your nose to pull out all your brains?"

I know, not the most mature conversation, but sometimes you have to fight fire with fire. Paul looks taken aback. Margaret usually ignores him.

"Stepped in any turds lately, Crapkate?" he finally tosses back.

"Does your face count?"

I grab Margaret and we sail away while his tiny brain tries to compute an answer. "He is such a jerk," I mutter.

I expect Margaret to agree, but she just shrugs. "I feel kind of sorry for him."

"Are you serious? He treats you like dirt. How can you feel sorry for him?"

Margaret straightens the hem of her sweater. "I heard his parents are divorced and his dad married someone else and moved away and"—she hesitates—"and they had a baby, but he never invites Paul to come see him."

I'm so surprised I can't think of a thing to say. It is kind of sad, I have to admit. Still, Margaret is way too mature for middle school. She should probably be in college somewhere.

The bell rings and I realize I only have five minutes to put my plan into motion and get to class. "Hey, did you leave your locker open?" I ask.

When Margaret glances back, I slip the note out of my

pocket and throw it on the floor. "Oh, look," I say casually. "What's that?"

Right on cue, Margaret scoops up the paper and reads it. "It looks like a note from Jake Knowles to Alyssa."

Margaret hesitates. Then she throws the note back on the floor and starts to walk away. This is definitely not according to my script.

"Uh, do you think she dropped it?" I say helpfully. "Maybe we should give it to her."

Margaret makes a face. "Not after the way she's treated you."

Margaret feels sorry for Paul Corbett but won't even hand off a note to Alyssa because she's been mean to me. I'm touched, but I'm also panicking. This scene seemed so easy when I wrote it, but real life is doing a major rewrite.

"That's true," I say, thinking fast. "But what if Jake's the one who dropped it? Maybe he meant to give it to Alyssa."

Margaret purses her lips. "You're right." She picks up the note.

I let loose a huge sigh of relief. Back on track.

"We should give it to Jake," Margaret says.

Wha-a-a? Not good. And then, who strolls down the hall toward us but Jake Knowles and his buddies? If I didn't know better, I'd say the hens were behind this.

"There he is," Margaret says brightly.

I'm desperate now. What would Tim Burton do? "He's with his friends," I blurt. "Don't you think he'll be embarrassed if we hand it to him in front of them? You know, since it's a note to a girl? They'll probably give him such a hard time."

Margaret turns and gazes at me, and I wonder if she's starting to suspect. The sweat on my face could be a clue.

"That is very thoughtful," she says, sounding like my mother.

I feel a twinge of shame that Margaret has such a high opinion of me. I remind myself that I'm doing this for her as well. "I don't want to do anything nice for Alyssa, either," I babble, "but I suppose for Jake's sake we should just give it to her." I hold my breath. Will she go for it?

Margaret shrugs. "Yeah, I guess. I'll give it to her in gym class."

Bingo. We're back on script. I wipe my face and hope that's the end of the ad-libbing.

The note handoff goes just as I expected. Alyssa looks surprised but does a good job of covering up after she reads the note. She stuffs it into her backpack, trying hard not to look excited. Alyssa has been waiting so long for Jake Knowles to notice her, and now she thinks he has. Well, the Beautiful Dame is in for a big letdown.

I'm finding it's a lot easier to carry out my plan if I think of Alyssa as the bad-to-the-bone Beautiful Dame. Not Alyssa, the girl with a secret crush, the climber of water towers. I don't really like calling her Beautiful Dame, either. It's too much like a compliment. I'll call her BD.

I shut my gym locker and turn away. BD has taken the bait, I tell myself. On to the next scene.

Halfway through fifth period I raise my hand and ask Mrs. Liebowitz, my Spanish teacher, if I can go to the nurse's office because I'm not feeling well.

She frowns. "No."

No? I sink back into my seat, stunned. What kind of heartless teacher keeps a sick kid in class? And why does a Spanish teacher have a name like *Liebowitz*, anyway? I'm starting to suspect the chickens have written their own script and sent it out into the cosmos, because nothing is going according to plan.

"Yo no te entiendo," Mrs. Liebowitz says, overemphasizing each syllable. She's spent so many years enunciating each vowel that she talks this way in English, too.

I sigh and rack my brain. *"Yo me siento bien,"* I finally manage. *I don't feel well.*

Mrs. Liebowitz beams at me. *"Muy bien, Katerina."* She nods at the door and I shoot out of class.

I hurry to the nurse's office and announce I have a major headache and can I lie down? Mrs. Stickney barely looks up as she waves me toward the cot. I wait ten minutes, then bounce up and announce I'm all better.

"Can I have a pass to get back to class?"

Mrs. Stickney, pleased at my quick recovery, hands me a pass.

I'm starting to feel a little like I'm in the middle of a

Mission: Impossible plotline, but without all the fancy gadgets. And without Tom Cruise. I return to Spanish class. When the bell rings, instead of going to my sixth-period class, I trail behind Alyssa as she hurries to the music classroom. Once she disappears inside, I quickly plant my second prop, and then I say a prayer. Mr. Cantrell has sixth period free. He usually stays in his office nearby, but he could decide to go to the teacher's lounge or even to the men's room. Considering how long my dad can camp out in the bathroom, this is a bleak thought.

I breathe a huge sigh of relief when I pass Mr. Cantrell's door. He's inside, humming to himself and conducting an invisible symphony. He looks so happy I feel sorry for him. He probably dreamed of being a world-famous conductor, and now he's stuck teaching pimply preteens in a suburban middle school. I make a note to myself to be nicer to Mr. Cantrell. Of course, if my plan backfires, I'll be at the top of his Most Hated Student list. A nasty case of doubt hits me like a bad bellyache. It's still not too late to ditch the plan. I suck in a deep breath and try to steady my nerves.

If I just picture what I'm doing as a movie shoot, it makes everything easier. After all, didn't Shakespeare say we're all just actors on a stage? Or maybe it was Jim Carrey. I try to ignore a nagging question, but it worms its way into my brain—does Alyssa really deserve this? I'm afraid of what the answer might be if I think about it too long. I've spent hours dreaming of this moment, and now it's already been set in motion. I think of Alyssa and Lydia laughing at their squiggle of Margaret and grit my teeth. I duck into the nearby bathroom and ease open the door so I can monitor the music room.

This next part is the trickiest. I have to guess how long Alyssa will wait for Jake before she gives up and goes to class. Five minutes feels like five hours. Suddenly, Miss Chell walks into the bathroom. I'm so startled I jump back and let out a hiccupy squeak.

Miss Chell teaches family and consumer education. Everyone calls her Miss Chill because she never smiles. Sure enough, she gives me a frosty look. "Do you have a pass?"

I quickly hold out the pass the nurse gave me. If Chilly reads it, my goose is cooked because the nurse wrote the time on it and that was half an hour ago. I've noticed, though, that most teachers don't bother to actually read the green slip. They just want to make sure you have one. Sure enough, Miss Chell purses her lips, then nods curtly and waves away the pass. I practically run out of the bathroom. What if Alyssa left while I wasn't looking?

She's still in the music room, rereading the note and looking fidgety. I race to Mr. Cantrell's office and burst through the door. "Mr. Cantrell, I've lost my mother's heirloom ring! I think I left it in the choir room this morning; have you seen it?"

He looks concerned. "Why, no, Kate, I haven't."

"She's going to kill me," I say in a choking voice. "It's really valuable. She'll be so upset if someone's taken it."

"Have you looked in the room yet?" he asks.

"Oh, thank you," I say, pretending to mishear him. "That would be so nice if you'd help me look. It's a pearl ring, a real pearl. She let me borrow it, and it must have slipped off my finger. . . ."

"I'm sure we'll find it." Mr. Cantrell stands up and we move into the hallway. No sign of Alyssa, which means she's still waiting for Jake.

"Wait!" I cry. "Wait, I think . . . maybe it wasn't the choir room after all. Maybe it was during gym class. I can't remember now."

"Well, it can't hurt to search the room, Kate. If we don't find it, you can go look in the gym."

"I don't want to waste your time."

"You're not wasting my time," Mr. Cantrell assures me.

Actually, I'm trying to buy time. I need to keep Mr. Cantrell in the hallway. Alyssa is in the music classroom. If we duck into the choir room two doors down, he won't see her leave. The little voice in my head has grown bigger and louder, and it's got lots more questions. What happened to that nice girl, Kate Walden? How did I ever think I was going to pull this off? Just because silly ideas succeed in movies doesn't mean they work in real life. . . .

And then, fate gives me a break. Alyssa bursts out of the music room. She stops short when she sees Mr. Cantrell.

"Why, Alyssa," he says, surprised. "What are you doing in there? Aren't you supposed to be in class?"

"Uh, yes, I was looking for something, but I couldn't find it," she blurts. Her face is turning ten shades of red. Only I know she's blushing because she was waiting for Jake Knowles and he stood her up. And the result is she looks guilty as sin as she hurries away, slinging her backpack over her shoulder.

"It seems everyone has lost something today," Mr. Cantrell muses. "Shall we look for your ring, Kate?"

"Oh my gosh, look, there it is!" I scoop up the ring I planted underneath the drinking fountain and wave it in front of Mr. Cantrell. It's a cheap dime store ring with a plastic pearl, so I'm hoping he won't look too closely.

He looks vaguely puzzled. "That was lucky. Be more careful next time."

"I will. Thanks, Mr. Cantrell!"

I duck into the bathroom until he goes back in his office. A part of me feels like crying and another part of me is completely amped, like I drank three Frappuccinos in a row. I take a deep breath and wipe my face. If that was the trickiest part, this next is the hardest.

I slip into the music room. It's so quiet I can hear the clock tick to the next minute. A fly buzzes along the window like a mini chain saw. I make my way over to the counter beneath the big windows. My heart is pounding in my ears like a cheesy sound effect from a second-rate horror flick. I swallow hard and glance nervously at the door. I've never taken school property before. If I'm caught, I'll be in big trouble.

I tell myself I'm only borrowing it, but my hand shakes as I grab the Cute Red Wig off its plastic head and stuff it into my backpack. I hurry outside and breathe a shaky sigh of relief. The hall is empty. I'm late to class and I get a tardy, but I don't even care. Relief washes over me as I slide into my seat. The deed is done. Excitement mixes with terror as I try not to look at my backpack. The trap is set. Now it's time for BD to take the fall.

18

The news spreads fast the next morning—the Cute Red Wig has been stolen. By the time Mr. Cantrell tells us in choir class, everybody already knows. He looks paler than normal, and I notice he gives Alyssa an extralong look. I was afraid Mr. Cantrell's music-soaked brain might not do the math, but it looks like he's put two and two together.

"Yes, it's true," he tells us. "Someone has taken the red wig for our *Annie* production. If anyone has information, I hope you will come to me. Otherwise, let's hope the thief comes to his—or her—senses and puts the wig back."

Everyone is glum, even Lydia. "This bites," she says loudly.

"Yeah," Alyssa agrees. "Who would want to steal the wig?"

"Who indeed?" Mr. Cantrell says quietly.

I wait for him to quiz Alyssa, but he doesn't say another word. Instead, he reaches for his songbook. Then it hits me. He'll probably question her in private. I feel like shaking him. Is this how Tim Burton feels when actors flub their lines? It looks like I'll have to take matters into my own hands.

"Hey, Alyssa, weren't you in the music room during sixth period yesterday?" I say, like it just occurred to me. "Remember, Mr. Cantrell? We were looking for my ring and we saw Alyssa. Did you see anything suspicious?" I ask innocently.

The entire room goes quiet. I almost hear the whirring brains as some of the kids remember that Alyssa hurried in late to English class, probably looking flustered.

Mr. Cantrell removes his glasses and rubs his eyes. "Yes, that's right. What were you doing in the room, Alyssa?"

Alyssa's face turns a sickly color. In a single second, she knows and I know and everyone else knows that she's become suspect *numero uno*, as Mrs. Liebowitz would say. "I wasn't doing anything," she stammers. "I was looking for a book I left."

"What book?" Mr. Cantrell asks.

And then, poor Alyssa's brain freezes. She gulps and hems and haws. All she needs to do is blurt out a title, any title, but she can't do it. "My English book," she finally manages.

"You had your English book in class yesterday," Jennifer Adams, our straight-A eager beaver pipes up. "We shared it, remember?"

"Yeah, I found it in the music room," Alyssa quickly covers. "The wig was still there when I left the room—I'm sure of it. I remember looking at it and thinking, 'Oh, the Cute Red Wig!'" She says it in a funny way and some of the girls chuckle. Alyssa's breathing easier now. She grins at Lydia, who says:

"Dang, you could have caught the criminal red-handed! You should have hid in the closet!"

Everyone laughs and settles into their chairs. Crisis averted.

I hold my breath. Mr. Cantrell is one of those old guys whose age is hard to figure out because he still has hair and he's still slender. He has to be in his forties, though. Does he have enough brain cells left to remember all the way back to yesterday, or has middle-age memory rot already kicked in? The clock ticks to the next minute.

Mr. Cantrell frowns and holds up a finger. Hallelujah. It's pointed at the ceiling, but an adjustment of a few degrees and it would be pointing at Alyssa. "You said yesterday that you didn't find what you were looking for in the music room."

You can almost feel the air get sucked out of the room. It's like we've suddenly been thrust into the middle of an old *Perry Mason* rerun, and Perry has just outfoxed the criminal

144

at the eleventh hour. As Alyssa looks like she's about to cry, a part of me feels sorry for her. I remind myself of the last week of torture, until *Crapkate* rings in my ears. I can't let my resolve crumble now.

"I didn't take it!" Alyssa babbles. "I swear I didn't!"

To a jury of adults, that sounds like a denial. A jury of seventh graders has way sharper ears. We know a clear admission of guilt when we hear one. Our legal reasoning goes something like this: people don't bother to deny something unless they've actually done it and therefore need to deny doing it.

This is where my superior scripting kicks in. Alyssa grabs her backpack and opens it. "See, I don't have it!"

Of course, no one expects her to be carrying the wig around in her backpack. Who would be that stupid? That's why I haven't bothered to plant the wig there. What I did plant on *top* of her backpack, as I passed behind her at the start of class, was a tiny curl of red hair that I yanked from the wig. To be honest, I didn't really expect a payoff from this, because Alyssa's backpack is dark and stuck under her chair. It wasn't likely anyone would notice, but I figured it couldn't hurt to try.

As Alyssa lifts her backpack to show everyone, the bright red curl slips onto the white linoleum like a bloody, crooked finger pointing right at Alyssa. Sometimes life does a better job scripting than I ever could.

"What is that?" Lydia shrieks. She picks up the curl and

holds it up. Even she is struck speechless. She finally flicks it at Alyssa. "Dude, just give the frickin' wig back."

The supreme court justice of seventh grade has spoken! The verdict: *Guilty*. Alyssa's goose is cooked.

"I didn't take it!" Alyssa insists again, but no one is listening.

Mr. Cantrell carefully picks up the red curl of hair, then motions for Alyssa to follow him. Her face is absolutely white and her lower lip trembles. She stands up and slowly follows him. Mr. Cantrell pauses at the door. "Jennifer, please lead the class in 'Oh My Heart' until I get back." He turns and Alyssa trails after him like a scolded puppy.

19

A good script has to be believable. Each plot development should make sense, like it could really happen. Alyssa dumping the wig in her locker just wasn't believable. Who's stupid enough to steal something and then put it in their locker, which can be searched? A lock of hair that accidentally ripped from the wig and stuck to her backpack—that was more believable. Plus, this way the wig is still missing. Therefore, people are still mad at Alyssa. Of course, I'll return the wig long before *Annie* is ready to hit the stage. I just want to let the resentment simmer a bit.

I find out later that the principal and Mr. Cantrell questioned Alyssa but she denied taking the wig. She had no idea how the lock of red hair got on her backpack. They asked to see her locker, but of course the wig wasn't there.

There's really no proof that she took it, so they finally let her go back to class. By then, almost the entire school has heard that *Alyssa Jensen took the Cute Red Wig and won't admit it.* All her denials only make it worse. Lydia pronounces her totally lame. She's toast.

And then it hits me: I've succeeded. Bogie has outwitted the Beautiful Dame. I go over and over the script in my head, amazed my crazy plan actually worked. Even the chickens couldn't mess it up. I spend the rest of the school day floating on a cloud. Lydia even comes up to me in the hallway and says, "Can you believe it? What is up with that chick?"

I guess she says it to me because I've been Alyssa's friend for so long. I notice Lydia already has a new BFF, Tina Turlick, who was her best friend for a while last year. At least Lydia recycles. Tina is one of her more rabid followers. She cut and colored her hair to look like Lydia's and she shops at all the same stores.

Tina makes a disgusted face. "She was probably just jealous because she knew you were going to get the part of Annie, Lydia. Mr. Cantrell practically said so. She couldn't handle it, so she took the stupid wig."

"Yeah, pretty lame," I agree. "She wasn't like that when we were friends." *She isn't like that now.* I squelch the tiny voice, but my stomach starts to hurt. I ignore it.

"It blows," Lydia says cheerfully. "So how's the zombie

movie coming, Mrs. Movie Director? When do I get to see my big scene?"

I freeze. Did I really throw the footage from Lydia's scenes into the trash? I rack my brain, trying to remember if I emptied the trash can on my desktop. I'm almost positive I didn't, which means I can still recover her scenes. Of course, there was hardly any useable footage, but maybe if I make it a really short scene...

"It looks great," I say, trying for enthusiasm. I feel a small thrill. Lydia isn't calling me *Crapkate*. She suddenly thinks my movie is cool enough to mention.

"Uh-oh," Lydia says. "Margaret Dorkel at three o'clock." She snaps her fingers. "Hey, maybe that hair on Alyssa's backpack was actually Margaret's! Check her hair and see if she's missing a chunk!"

Tina grins. "We could shave Margaret's head and make a new wig."

I can see Margaret's smile falter as she approaches us. Twelve-year-old girls have a built-in sonar that can detect when they're being talked about from a quarter mile away. I stifle a desire to slap Lydia and Tina.

It doesn't seem fair that they love the Cute Red Wig but make fun of Margaret's hair. Why is being a ginger adorable in a musical but joke material in real life? There are other redheads in school who don't get teased like Margaret. So I guess part of Margaret's problem is that she's a Henrietta.

Except where Henrietta is too timid, Margaret is just too nice. Anyway, she can't help it if she has bright red hair. And messed-up teeth are just genetics. What can she do about that except beg her parents for braces?

Margaret gave me a seat in the lunchroom. She acted like a friend when even my BFF ignored me. Lydia didn't do any of that. And then I realize, Lydia might be funny but she's careless. She makes everything a joke so no one can accuse her of being mean. And maybe everything is just a big joke to her, but it isn't to me. And now, a couple words from Lydia and I'm practically drooling on the floor. Maybe I should slap myself.

"Hey, Margaret," I say loudly. "How's it going?"

"Hi." Margaret shoots a quick glance my way. "That's strange about the wig, isn't it? Maybe whoever took it will put it back."

"We shouldn't wait," Lydia says. "Let's go raid Alyssa's closet. I bet she's got the wig stashed with her dirty laundry."

Tina wrinkles her nose. "Yuck. It would be like putting dirty underwear on your head."

"You did that the last time you were at my house!" Lydia shrieks. "You should have seen her! She grabbed my underwear and stuck it on top of her head and went running around the house! My brother thought she was on drugs!"

"I did not!" Tina screams. "They were clean!"

"Are you kidding? Nothing on my floor is clean!"

"You put underwear on your head, too!"

"At least it's my own, moron."

By this time they're both cracking up. Mr. Brumberg, one of the science teachers, appears at his door and frowns. "Hello, Mr. Brumby," Lydia sings out. She has a nickname for almost every teacher. The weird thing is, none of them seem to mind.

"Don't you girls need to go to class?" he inquires.

"We're cutting class," Lydia informs him. "We thought we'd stand outside your door and entertain you today."

Mr. Brumberg lips twitch. "Move along, Lydia."

"Okay, Mr. Brumby, whatever you say!"

Lydia and Tina amble off and I try to get away fast, too, because I'm pretty sure I know what Margaret wants to talk about.

But she's too quick. "What do you think about Alyssa?"

I shrug. Low-key is best. "I don't know, it's pretty weird."

"I wonder if Jake Knowles ever showed up in the music room." Her voice sounds doubtful. Has she figured it out?

If Margaret asks Jake about the note he never wrote, I'm in trouble. "You should ask him," I say casually, because I'm pretty sure she won't. Jake Knowles is supercute and athletic. I doubt even Margaret wants to ask him if he stood up Alyssa. She shrugs like it's no big deal, and relief washes over me. She doesn't suspect anything.

I hurry off to my last class of the day, feeling like I'm some kind of mysterious Beautiful Dame myself. I've outfoxed them all. I turn a corner and almost run into Alyssa.

She turns her tearstained face away and hurries outside, where I can see her mother's car waiting. It's so bad she's leaving school early.

I swallow hard as the car pulls away. *Serves her right*, I tell myself. *Now she knows how it feels.* But suddenly I don't feel nearly so beautiful.

20

My mother must have told my dad about our little talk because after he gets home from work, he finds me in the TV room. I've already hidden the wig in my closet. I changed the hiding place three times and I'm still worried my mother will find it. It makes me so nervous I can barely focus on the TV show. I don't think Margaret suspects anything, but what if she starts to piece things together? What if Alyssa figures it out? After all, I'm the one who pointed the finger at her. I just wanted to borrow the wig for a couple of weeks to make people mad at her. No big deal, right? But suddenly it does feel like a very big deal.

And what would my parents think about what I did? A chill runs through me. My dad always lectures Derek and me about how some kids take the wrong path in life and end up as deadbeats, and how we have to be careful not to do that. Is this what he means? Am I a future deadbeat?

My dad claps his hands together and gives me a big smile. "So, are you shooting another scene for your movie this weekend? Who's the zombie this time?"

I stare at the TV. "I'm not working on that anymore."

My dad looks pretend surprised. "You mean you've finished it? That's great!"

I yank a big pillow onto my lap and sink my chin onto it. "No, I deleted the whole thing. It was fun to work on when I was little, but now it's just kind of stupid."

That's a big, fat lie. I hadn't really thought about deleting my movie until that second. It sure gets my dad's attention, though. Lately, I seem addicted to saying whatever will hurt or scare my parents the most. I'm not sure why. I guess, deep down, I kind of like the attention, even though I pretend not to.

His face actually goes pale. "You deleted it?" he repeats. He collapses in a chair. "Kate, are you serious?"

"Well, I'm going to delete it," I mutter, "as soon as I go upstairs."

My dad gives a big sigh of relief. It's nice to know *he* cares about my movie, at least.

"Kate, you've worked so hard on *Night of the Zombie Chickens* and it's almost done. Why would you want to throw it all away? And wouldn't Alyssa be mad if you did that?"

Now he's fishing. My mother has clearly debriefed him. I shrug. "Alyssa could not care less."

He quietly nods. "Did you girls have a fight?"

I pretend to be fascinated by SpongeBob SquarePants on TV, even though I've seen the episode three times already. "It doesn't matter."

Of course it matters, as in life or death. My dad's not stupid. He leans forward. "You want to talk about it?"

I shake my head. I used to be such a tough kid. Hardly anything made me cry. I cried when our cat got run over. I cried when I fell out of a tree and broke my wrist. Otherwise, I pretty much sucked it up. Now, just hearing the worry in my dad's voice brings tears to my eyes. A big part of me wants to blubber on his shoulder and say dumb things like, "What is going on?" Or maybe, "What did I do wrong?"

But I can't. I can't even quite look him in the eye, because I'm afraid he'll somehow read the truth in my face. Now that I've taken the Cute Red Wig and gotten Alyssa in trouble, I feel like I'm perched at the top of a slippery hill, with a huge swamp of mud at the bottom. And it feels like I'm sliding down inch by inch.

Anyway, how can I trust my father enough to cry on his shoulder when he's keeping a secret from us? All I can think of is Lydia's dad and how he lied to his whole family until he got caught. I feel guilty for even thinking my dad might do something like that. But what if he is?

He stands up and tousles my hair. "If you decide you want to talk, I'll be in the den. I, uh..." He hesitates. "I need to make some phone calls."

I nod, staring as hard as I can at the TV. More phone calls. No, I definitely can't talk to my dad.

He pauses at the door. "Just do me one favor. Promise me you won't delete the movie. No need to be in a rush. You don't want to do something you might regret later."

I give a big, noisy sigh. "Okay, fine."

A couple of minutes after my dad leaves, Derek shows up. He plops down in a chair and stares at me like I'm a lab specimen. "What's the matter with you?"

"What are you talking about?"

"You've been acting weird lately. And mom says you had a fight with Alyssa and you're not working on your movie anymore."

I sit up straight. "She told you that?"

"Kind of. I overheard her talking about it with Dad."

I give him a withering look. "You should stop listening at doors."

Derek shrugs. "So is it true? Did you guys have a fight?"

I eye him suspiciously. Sometimes, Derek and I get along fine. But other times, he calls me names and teases me and takes junk out of my room and bugs me until I want to scream. So usually I do. At him. Then, we both get in trouble.

"What do you care?"

"Sheesh, I was just wondering. You don't have to bite my head off. Alyssa's a dumb butt anyway. And that girl that played your last zombie? I had to put earplugs in, she was so loud. She couldn't even act."

"How do you know?"

"I was watching from the window upstairs. She was running around, screaming like an idiot."

I smile a little, despite myself. He's right; Lydia and Alyssa are just two loud, dumb-butt girls. "Yeah, she was pretty bad," I agree.

I steal a glance at Derek. He was watching us from a window? Boy, he must have been really bored. Sometimes I forget that living way out here also affects him. Maybe that's why he's always bugging me, asking to help with my movie.

"Wanna play Mario?" Derek asks.

"Sure."

I'm a little touched when he gives me a big grin and jumps up to plug it in. He seems pretty excited just because I'm going to play video games with him. "Prepare to get creamed," I advise him.

"In your dreams," he retorts.

We grin at each other as he throws me a remote. It feels good to have a truce with one person in my life, even if I know it can't last.

21

My plan has worked better than I could have imagined—
or worse than I could have dreamed, depending on how
you look at it. The next day, kids start heckling Alyssa in the
hallway. "Where's the wig, Jensen?" People stare at her as
she walks by. Lydia and her crew ignore her. Alyssa doesn't
even show up in the lunchroom, which means she's probably
hiding in a bathroom stall, crying and eating her sandwich.

I keep telling myself that she's learning a valuable lesson. No pain, no gain. You need to walk a mile in someone
else's shoes.

It seems like everybody wants to talk about it. Even
Margaret shakes her head at lunch and murmurs, "Poor
Alyssa. I wonder why she took it."

She glances sideways at me, and for a moment I'm sure

she's guessed everything. Then I decide she's just waiting for me to say something.

"Took what?" Doris asks. She glances up from her biology book and shoves a potato chip in her mouth. Doris's mind must be like an underground cave, vast and soundproof. Nothing sinks in unless it sounds scientific.

Sighing noisily, I reach over and slam shut her book. Anything to change the subject. "Doris, you cannot study during lunch hour."

Her forehead wrinkles. "Why not?"

"Doris, look around you. Do you see a single other person with a book open?"

She peers around, still frowning.

"Lunch is for socializing," I go on. "You're supposed to talk to people. Have fun."

"No one wants to talk to me."

She says it matter-of-factly. A few weeks ago I would have shrugged it off, but now she can't fool me. I know how much work it takes to convince yourself and everyone else that being ignored doesn't bother you.

I mock glare at her. "Why do you think Margaret and I are sitting here?"

"Because you don't have anywhere else to sit." Her voice is so calm it makes my insides hurt—for Doris and myself and all the other girls who have to pretend it doesn't hurt and that we don't care.

Margaret inhales sharply. "Doris, how can you say that?"

"Yeah, Doris, thanks a lot." My voice comes out weak. I'm ashamed that there's a little bit of truth in what she said.

"Okay, fine." Doris shoves up her glasses. "Sorry. I can still talk and study my book at the same time."

I realize suddenly that it's not about studying. I'm taking Doris's security blanket away. She doesn't know what to do without a book nearby. It's her escape when things get uncomfortable.

Still, sometimes we all need hard medicine. Doris has been helping me a lot with my math homework. Now I'm going to return the favor. Welcome to Social Skills 101.

"When you're staring into a book," I say slowly, "it makes it seem like you don't care. Like you're not listening. And usually you're *not* listening."

"Yes I am!"

"Then how come you're the only one in the entire school who doesn't know that Alyssa Jensen took the..." I flinch inwardly but force out the words. "That she stole the Cute Red Wig?"

Doris's eyes grow large. "She stole the wig?"

"Well, she maybe took it," Margaret says carefully. "You're innocent until proved guilty, right, Kate?"

Margaret is starting to unnerve me.

"So no more books at lunch," I go on, ignoring her. "Trust me, Doris, you're plenty smart already."

Doris shrugs. "Okay, so what should we talk about?"

We all stare at each other. Nothing kills a conversation faster than asking that question.

"You know, I really feel like seeing a movie," Margaret says. "I love movies." She shoots a sideways glance at me and I know immediately what's going on.

What Margaret's really doing is asking if I want to see a movie. If I sound enthusiastic, then she'll figure it's safe to suggest we go see one. If I ignore what she said or change the subject, then she'll drop it. Since she didn't ask and I didn't say no, we avoid all the awkwardness. I have to hand it to Margaret; she understands how to say stuff by not saying it. Unlike Doris.

"Yeah, let's go see a movie Friday night," Doris blurts. "I heard *Poisoned Pie* is playing at the Westmark. You guys want to go?"

If it's not in an equation, Doris doesn't get it.

"Uh, *Poisoned Pie*? I don't think I've heard of that." I sip on the organic apple juice my mother packed in my lunch, trying to buy time. If I go to a movie with them, will it cement my low social standing forever? I like Margaret and Doris, but I have to be honest with myself, too. I don't want to be unpopular. I don't want to be the butt of mean jokes. I don't want Paul Corbett and Blake Nash calling me *Crap-kate* all through high school.

My head swirls and suddenly I'm bone tired. My life feels like a chess game where I have to figure out what move to make five turns in advance. I'm sick of worrying about who's my friend and who's not, and what people are saying about me. I'm sick of pretending to ignore Alyssa while watching her from the corner of my eye. It's all too much work. Besides, I haven't done a single fun thing in weeks.

"Sure," I say loudly. "Why not? Let's go to a movie."

Margaret beams at me, and even Doris lifts her upper lip a fraction.

I wish I could say I feel great, but I don't. The organic apple juice is already turning into vinegar in my stomach.

22

Our boring suburban town is like every other boring suburban town in the U.S. It has a long street crammed full of fast-food joints, chain motels, gas stations, and bowling alleys. The Westmark Theater sits like a fake crown jewel in the middle of all these McFoods and McSleeps. It has a fancy marquee that glows red and yellow, with the name *Westmark* lit by hundreds of little bulbs. A few of the bulbs in the "A" burned out once, so for a while it read *Westmurk*. It was such a perfect name for a horror flick that I shot footage of the sign one night before they got around to fixing it. I'm saving it for my next movie. At least, I was. That was back when I thought *Night of the Zombie Chickens* might have a sequel.

I end up arriving late, which is only semi on purpose, so the lobby is almost empty. We quickly buy our tickets and popcorn and slip into the theater. The trailers have already started, so we stumble to our seats in the dark. I scrunch down, feeling the familiar tingle of excitement I get whenever I see a movie. I always pay attention to who's directing it and I usually tell myself, "One day that will be my name," but now I just look away and noisily slurp on my soda.

It feels funny not working on my movie anymore. Sometimes, I still catch myself worrying about the ending. I have to remind myself it doesn't matter, and then I get this funny feeling, like someone poked a hole in my stomach and forgot to plug it.

Luckily, movies are great for making you forget your problems. I take a big handful of popcorn and stuff it in my mouth as the opening credits roll.

Poisoned Pie is rated PG-13 so, depending on the person, it's kind of scary or it's kind of funny. It's about a woman who owns a bakery and makes fantastic pies. Everybody in town is crazy about them. But then she moves her business out of her home and into an old warehouse on the edge of town. Suddenly, weird things start happening. A woman bites into an apple pie and winds up with a piece of intestine dangling from her mouth. A greedy little boy sticks his whole face into a pie, only the filling turns out to be bloody, not cherry. The blood is definitely top quality, I'll give them that. As I watch it ooze off the screaming boy's face, I can't help wondering what ingredients they used to give it such a slick shine.

I quickly learn that Margaret is a screamer and Doris is a laugher. It's the first time I've heard Doris laugh, and at first I think she's trying to be creepy to go along with the movie, but it turns out that really is how she laughs. So when something scary happens, Margaret screams and Doris makes a sound like a goose with a head cold. That sets me off giggling. Margaret leans over and nudges me.

"Don't you think it's scary?"

"Sure," I say, trying to sound like I mean it. The truth is, I can only give it a C-plus on my fear factor scale.

"What are you laughing at?" she whispers.

I bite my lip. Suddenly, Doris lets loose with another cackle. I can't help it, I start giggling again. Margaret looks at Doris, then back at me. Pretty soon she's giggling, too, and then we're all laughing so loud that we almost get kicked out.

At the end of the movie I scan the audience, more out of habit than anything. Nobody there I know. We play a few arcade games in the lobby and then decide to walk over to Twisters, a burger-and-ice-cream joint. I know there's a good chance we'll be spotted, but I'm starving and I don't care. It's strange, but all those things that we used to poke fun at—Margaret's red hair and crooked teeth,

Doris's lumpy brown clothes and deadpan voice—I hardly even notice now. What I notice more is Margaret's funny, oddball humor, or how Doris will explain math homework three times over until I get it. I must seem like a mental slug to her, but she never laughs when I mess up. She just pushes up her glasses and starts explaining all over again.

"I felt so sorry for Nadine, the baker," Margaret says as we lounge in a booth. "When she found that dead body, I thought she was going to flip out and start chopping it up."

"Yeah, that was funny," Doris says. "But that time portal the undead janitor used?" She shakes her head. "Their explanation of dark energy was totally inaccurate."

I think about it. "They had good blood," I say at last.

Doris starts cackling, and that sets off me and Margaret. I take a bite of my burger as Doris noisily sucks up the last of her soda. At that moment, Alyssa walks in with her mother. For a split second, Alyssa's eyes lock with mine and then we both quickly look away. I feel a rush of blood rising up my neck and into my face. Doris is still loudly sucking up drops from the bottom of her glass. I'm tempted to grab the straw and tie it in a knot. I wish Alyssa had come in a moment earlier when we were all laughing.

"There's Alyssa," Doris says in her deadpan voice.

Margaret glances over her shoulder. All the tables in front of us are full, which means Alyssa and her mother will have to walk right by us toward the back. My heart starts to pound. Mrs. Jensen will probably stop and ask why I haven't been over to the house lately. Alyssa is probably already embarrassed that we saw her come in with her mother. Clearly, no one wants to hang with her. What if her mother suggests they sit with us?

Talk about awkward. I stuff a french fry in my mouth, trying to think of what to do.

"I heard you're making a movie, Kate," I dimly hear Margaret say. "Something about zombies?"

Doris pauses. "Really?"

Then, a true miracle. An old couple up front stands to leave. As I watch Alyssa and her mother slide into their booth, something squeezes my heart. This was Alyssa's and my favorite place to eat.

"Kate?"

I turn back to Margaret, my mind hazy. "Huh?"

"You're making a movie?" she prompts.

"I was. But..." I sip my drink. "I lost interest. It's kind of stupid. I mean, it's not like anyone would want to see it."

"You're making a movie?" Doris repeats. "Wow. That's really..." She trails off and slurps noisily on her soda again.

I can't help wondering what she thinks it is—weird, stupid, unscientific?

Margaret looks slightly horrified, like I just said I was having a body part amputated. She leans forward and actually grips the table.

"It's not stupid. I mean, if it's something you love, then you should stick with it." Her voice rises a notch. "Don't let other people talk you out of going after what you want."

When I stare at her, she blushes and mumbles, "That's what my mother always tells me."

I never thought about Margaret *going after* something. She always seems so quiet. I'm about to ask what it is she wants when Doris finally gives up on finding another drop of liquid at the bottom of her drink.

"I think making a movie is really..." She tips the cup into her mouth and chews on a mouthful of melting ice—*crunch crunch crunch*. "It's really impressive."

I glance at her, surprised. That isn't the word I was expecting.

"You don't think it's lame?"

"Are you kidding?" Margaret gazes at me through her round glasses. "I don't know anyone our age who's doing something that cool."

And then I feel it, a catch in my throat, the early warning signal for tears on the way. Unbelievable. I stuff a handful of fries in my mouth and focus on the delicious, hot, salty grease. It works; the tears back off. Still, it feels like Doris's and Margaret's words have jarred something loose inside me. Maybe I am giving up too easily. If I quit just because people make fun of it, then it's like they've won somehow. They're telling me what I should or shouldn't do. And I hate it when people tell me what to do.

I smile at Margaret. "Maybe you're right." Inside, my heart is soaring at the thought that my movie might not be dead. Then, I remember—I have no star and no ending.

"Margaret is always right," Doris says matter-of-factly. "Except in her choice of reading material."

Trust Doris to have the last, bizarre word. It feels good to all laugh together, until Alyssa turns and glances our way. My smile fades and I can't help wondering if maybe she thinks we're laughing at her.

23

All weekend, I think about Margaret's comments about my movie. On Sunday night, I open up my movie project on my computer, click on a random clip, and wait for it to open in the viewer. It turns out to be some footage of the hens I shot last summer, trying to get some zombielike behavior. First, a hen pecks at the ground. I can hear Alyssa in the background, snapping her fingers. She was behind me, trying to get the hen to look up toward the camera.

"Here, chickie, chickie," she calls. "Chicka chicka boom boom."

The hen ignores her.

"Hey, beakface, look over here!" Alyssa shouts. The hen skitters away. The camera is shaking because I'm laughing.

Alyssa runs into frame and chases the hen, shouting, "Look over here, you stupid bird!" The frazzled hen bolts for the coop and Alyssa collapses on the ground. I stand over her, shooting down. She throws a handful of grass up at the camera and it falls back in her face. She spits some out of her mouth.

"You're probably lying in chicken poop," I hear myself tell her.

She screams and jumps up, the camera jerks wildly, and the shot ends.

It's nothing special, but I watch it again anyway. When I feel myself wanting to watch it a third time, I know I have to snap out of it. I take a deep breath. There's nothing useable in the clip, so I make myself delete it. That little snippet of electronic memory is gone forever. It's like it never existed, like Alyssa and I never chased chickens and laughed and did silly things last summer.

What is Alyssa doing right now? Is she dreading school tomorrow? Is she begging her mother to let her stay home?

I stare at the closet. How soon should I return the wig?

I wish I could just run to the school that night, slip in, and put it back. I'm tired of the whole wig drama. I thought I would feel better once I taught Alyssa a lesson, but I don't. I feel worse. And when I wrote my plan, I didn't think about how I would return the wig. I figured it would be easy, but now I'm not so sure. What if someone catches me?

I tell myself it isn't quite time to put it back yet. What I really need to do is focus on something else. Anything else. I decide the moment has arrived to finally come up with an ending for my movie. Any kind of creative thinking requires food, so I wander downstairs to find supplies. Wilma follows me, probably hoping I'll give her a snack. As I pass the den, I can hear my dad talking on the phone again. Suddenly, he gives a low laugh. A private laugh.

The hairs on the back of my neck feel like a cold hand just brushed over them. I try to listen at the door, but it's a solid piece of farmhouse wood and all I can hear is the low murmur of his voice. Wilma barks once, trying to get my attention. My dad's voice stops short. I grab Wilma and race back upstairs, my appetite gone. I peek into my parents' room. My mother is sitting in bed with her glasses on, going over some paperwork. Waiting for my dad.

I slip away before she sees me and park myself in front of my computer. When I Google *midlife crisis*, it says that middle-aged men and women sometimes feel trapped by money worries and family problems. They crave change and excitement. They want new, more fulfilling relationships. They buy expensive toys to make themselves feel young.

Money worries and family problems. I jab the delete button. My dad probably feels like he has both. Money is tight, my mother's always busy with her hens, Derek and I bicker too much, the house always needs repairs. . . . The list goes on and on.

I wander out to the hallway and sink onto the top stair, still clutching Wilma. My problems with Alyssa suddenly don't seem so important. I need to know who my dad is talking to every night. I can't live anymore with this fear in the pit of my stomach. I need to know if my dad is the guy I think he is, or if he's just pretending to be that guy. If only I had a pair of Extendable Ears, like the Weasley twins invented in *Harry Potter and the Order of the Phoenix*. I sigh as Wilma licks my face, trying to help.

Suddenly, I hear the door to my dad's office creak open. I bolt into my room with Wilma, shut the door, and turn off the light. He slowly climbs the stairs and, a moment later, their bedroom door clicks shut. I huddle in the dark, feeling miserable. Wilma licks my ear, and that's when it hits me. I may not have magical ears, but I have the next best thing. If I can just find a certain item, I'll be able to hear everything my dad says in his office. The problem is, I'm pretty sure my mother stored that item in the basement.

I try to persuade myself to look for it in the morning. After all, it's too late to spy on my dad tonight. I can't wait, though. Patience isn't one of my virtues. I remember seeing the item years ago, stored with a bunch of Derek's and my old toys and books. It was all useless stuff and I wondered at the time why my mother kept it. Did she finally throw that box away when we moved?

I ease open my door.

"Sorry, Wilma," I whisper. "You need to stay here." She

gives me a mournful look as I shut the door. The last thing I need is for her to sniff a mouse in the basement and start yapping. I slip downstairs and find a flashlight.

I click on the basement light and gaze at the curved wooden stairs disappearing into the abyss. The flashlight is just in case. If the electricity goes off or Derek is secretly stalking me and decides to shut off the lights, I want to be ready. I feel like I've stepped into a weird horror flick. All I need is my own creepy sound track.

To take my mind off the cobwebs and the rats and the dead-person smell, I hum a few eerie notes as I descend step by step. I stop when I hear a scuttling noise under the stairs. Maybe I *should* wait until morning. Whatever it was, it sounded big. At the shadowy far end of the basement, I can see plastic bins stacked high. Humming louder, I jump the last few steps and streak past the water heater and the rusty oil tank. Then, the sump pump gurgles at me and I freeze. I've heard stories about people losing tiny baby pet snakes in their houses, only to have them show up years later, six feet long and fat as fire hydrants. What if there's a viper curled up in the sump pump?

I switch gears and start humming Harry Potter's theme music. If he could deal with snakes, then so can I. I rush past the sump pump, my heart jumping wildly.

Only the furnace and the cistern stand between me and the bins. The furnace is mammoth, with big metal octopus arms that reach into the ceiling. Just like in *Home Alone*. I think of little Macaulay Culkin standing up to his monster furnace, and I even manage to kick ours as I hurry past it. Bad idea. A metallic booming sound fills the basement and echoes off the walls. I gasp, sure my dad will come running. Or worse, Wilma will start barking upstairs. I listen, but there's no barking, no running feet. Sometimes, heavy old farmhouse walls come in handy.

The wall of the cistern is just high enough that I can't see over it. Anything could be in there—rats, dead bodies, vampires, zombie chickens. It's the creepiest part of the whole basement, steeped in shadowy evil. Even Macaulay Culkin didn't have to deal with a cistern. I'm trapped— cistern in front of me, and monster furnace and viper sump pump behind. My heart is pounding crazily. *It's my house,* I tell myself. *It's my basement. Nothing's in here waiting to grab me. Nothing wants to suck my blood. Nothing wants to tear out my organs. . . .*

Okay, that pep talk's not working.

I lean down, trying to think, and notice my shoelace is coming untied. My Nike shoelace. I close my eyes. *Just do it. JUST DO IT!*

I streak forward. From the corner of my eye, I'm sure I see something reach from the cistern and grab at my hair as I run past. *Just do it just do it just do it. . . .*

I reach the bins and wheel around, the flashlight raised over my head like a weapon. Nothing. Still, I lift the first lid without turning my back on the empty room. Nothing's

175

going to sneak up on me if I can help it. A quick glance tells me it's Christmas stuff. I open the next box. Winter hats and gloves. I push that box aside and open the one underneath it. Christmas again. This could take a while.

On the sixth box, I hit gold. My old Cabbage Patch doll stares up at me. I'd forgotten how cute she was. There's Derek's first pair of shoes, and my favorite cardboard picture book, *I Can Fly*. It would be nice to reminisce about old times, but I can't help thinking about that undead janitor and his time portal in *Poisoned Pie*. Suddenly, that movie doesn't seem quite so funny.

I glimpse a white cord and grab it. With a hard yank, the item tumbles out of the bin. *Bingo*. I hold it up to the light and inspect it. Derek's baby monitor. I vaguely remember listening to him scream through it. He was a noisy baby. I dig down and uncover the white plastic base. *Mission: Impossible* accomplished.

I restack the bins, then dash forward in an all-out, record-breaking sprint. I don't slow down until I am all the way upstairs safely underneath the covers in my bedroom.

When Lydia's loud giggle drifts over from a nearby table, I stifle a desire to throw my lunch at her. How can one person find that many things to laugh at? She belongs in India. She would have the biggest laugh club of them all.

Next to me, Margaret peels an egg and takes a bite. Hard-boiled eggs smell even worse than fried eggs, if that's possible. I hunch miserably in my seat and stare at my sandwich. I'm still scarred from my midnight stealth operation in the basement. Even worse, now I have to spy on my dad. How low is that? I'm afraid of what I might hear, but I'm even more afraid of what happened to Lydia and Alyssa—believing everything was fine right up until their dads moved out.

Margaret dabs a yellow crumb from her mouth and brushes the eggshells into her paper bag. It occurs to me that if nature had simply given Margaret brown hair and fewer freckles, she might be sitting at a table full of girls right now. And who knows? If Lydia had been born with red hair and bad eyesight, maybe she would be the one hanging out with me and Doris. It all seems so unfair. If only there were mutant eggs that could change hair color. Now, *that* would be a big seller. Forget organic. If my mother could sell eggs like that, we'd be rich. Margaret would probably be first in line.

Just as I take a bite of my chocolate cupcake, an idea hits me with the force of a Supertronic laser stun gun. MUTANT EGGS. Of course! Why didn't I think of it before?

The ending of my movie is staring me right in the face. I don't need Alyssa at all. I'm so shocked that I can't even chew. All these weeks of struggle, all my writing and rewriting, even Alyssa's betrayal—for the moment, none of it matters. I turn to Margaret and Doris to break the amazing news, and that's when I realize my idea has one huge problem. My new ending requires a new star. Right now, my talent pool consists of Margaret and Doris. I sneak a glance at Doris. If I brushed out her hair and got rid of the glasses...

"Um, Doris..." I'm so nervous about asking that I

accidentally drop my organic chocolate, all-natural cupcake. It lands on the table, frosting side down.

"You going to eat that?" Doris asks me.

I stare at the chocolate frosting flattened on the dirty, grungy lunchroom table and shake my head. She grabs it and takes a huge bite, and then she *wipes her finger along the smeared frosting on the table and pops it in her mouth*. I think I might be sick. Margaret is staring very hard at the clock on the wall. I feel a twinge of sympathy for a neat freak like her, hanging around with a slobaholic like Doris.

"What were you going to ask me?" Doris spews cupcake crumbs as she speaks, and *one lands in my drink*. I couldn't have written a better gross-out scene if I'd tried.

"Uh, nothing." I try not to look at the floatie in my soda. Social Skills 101 may be a little too advanced for Doris.

I weakly turn and regard Margaret. Her hair glows nearly orange in the fluorescent lights. She smiles at me, showing all her crooked teeth. I smile back. *Night of the Zombie Chickens* has a new star.

Margaret and Doris agree to come over on Saturday to shoot the final scene of my movie. That morning, my mother bustles around acting cheerful. Things are still strained between us. I catch her watching me sometimes. I'm watching my dad, and Derek is listening in on all of us. It's like we're all spies, trying to decipher one another's secret code.

"How about cookies?" my mother asks. "Would you like me to make cookies for your friends?"

"No," I say, a little too quickly. "No, thanks."

Margaret and Doris arrive together. "I didn't know you have chickens," Doris says as soon as I open the door. I feel like asking her what school she goes to, or for that matter, what planet she lives on. But that's just Doris. The entire world could be talking about chicken poop and she'd be too busy doing algebra problems to notice.

"Hello, Kate. Hello, Mrs. Walden." Margaret is all formal politeness. She actually shakes my mother's hand. "This is a lovely house," Margaret tells her. If it were anyone else, I'd say this was some serious sucking up, but Margaret actually seems to mean it. "I love farmhouses," she goes on, "especially with gables, like yours. It reminds me of *Anne of Green Gables*."

I don't even know what a gable is, but I can tell from my mother's face that I'm going to hear an earful later about Margaret's delightful manners. "And look at that!" she goes on, pointing to the hideous rooster border. "It's adorable!"

"Margaret!" I yelp, and shove the script in her face. "Here's the script. Read it over. Doris, you should read it, too." Doris is going to be one of my final zombies, along with Derek and his friend.

"This is probably the toughest scene I've had to write," I tell them, biting a nail. Having other people read my writing always makes me nervous. And this was a rush job—I stayed up late finishing it the night before. This is what I came up with:

```
INT: MALLORY'S HOUSE—WINTER DAY


Mallory runs into the house. She
wears a winter coat and a ski mask so
her face is HIDDEN.
```

MALLORY
(to herself)
What am I going to do? I haven't
eaten in three days and there's
no food left in the cupboards.
This is the only food I found.

She pulls an egg from her pocket.

MALLORY
If I eat this egg, I'll turn
into a zombie. But I don't care
anymore. I'm so hungry I have to
eat something. And this house is
so cold I don't even want to take
off my ski mask.

INT: KITCHEN—CONTINUOUS

Mallory fills a pot with water,
tosses the egg inside, and puts it on
the stove.

CUT TO:

Mallory, still in coat and ski mask,
peels the egg. She's about to take a

bite when sudden BANGING at the door
makes her stop. She backs away from
the door.

                    MALLORY
          They're back. They're never
          going to leave me alone! I might
          as well just become one of
          them!

She runs toward the basement door.

INT: BASEMENT

Mallory bolts the basement door,
then slowly walks down the steps.
The BANGING grows nearer—from the
basement door. She backs into a
corner and holds up the egg.

                    MALLORY
          I've held out for so long, but
          now the only thing left is to
          eat this poisoned egg. Curse
          those zombie chickens! They took
          my family and friends, and now
          they're going to take me.

Mallory wipes away a tear and takes
a bite. She makes a CHOKING noise
and grabs her throat. The light
flickers on and off. The house shakes
like there's an EARTHQUAKE. Mallory
GROANS and collapses as the basement
goes black.

CUT TO:

The light flickers back on. Mallory
staggers to her feet. She slowly
pulls off the face mask to reveal . . .
A NEW FACE! Mallory is now a REDHEAD
with FRECKLES! She feels her face.

                    MALLORY
            I feel so strange . . . so
            different. What's happened to me?

She finds an old hand mirror in the
basement, looks into it, and GASPS.

                    MALLORY
            I look like a different person!
            But how can it be? How come I'm
            not a zombie?

She SCREAMS at the sound of
SPLINTERING wood. The zombies have
busted down the door, and now three
of them descend the basement stairs.

MALLORY
They found me! Now I'm going to
be a meal for the zombies. Why
does it have to end like
this?

The zombies lurch toward her, hands
outstretched. Mallory SCREAMS and
covers her face. The zombies stop and
bow low.

ZOMBIES
All hail the Zombie Queen!

Mallory peeks through her fingers.

MALLORY
Huh?

HEAD ZOMBIE
She has eaten an egg of the
Zombie World and survived!

She is the new Zombie Queen!
All hail the Zombie Queen!

The zombies make way for
Mallory.

> MALLORY
> This is weird. I can suddenly
> understand them. So you're not
> going to eat me?

> HEAD ZOMBIE
> No zombie will harm you. You are
> free to roam the world, and we
> will protect you!

> ZOMBIES
> All hail the Zombie Queen!

> MALLORY
> Wow. That's so amazing.
> A new face and a new
> life!

Mallory climbs the basement
stairs.

EXT: MALLORY'S HOUSE—DAY

> MALLORY
> Look, all the snow melted. It's
> like summer suddenly. And now
> I'm free to roam the world and
> go wherever I want without
> ever worrying about zombies
> again! Thank you, zombie
> chickens!

Mallory walks off down the country
road, silhouetted by the FLAMING RED
setting sun.

THE END

I'm a little nervous as Margaret reads it over. Will she think it's silly? I feel like explaining that it's not easy being a twelve-year-old director. I mean, how many directors have to do their math homework before they can work on their script? When Margaret finishes, her face looks solemn and I'm afraid she's going to say she hates it or she's morally opposed to eating zombie eggs.

Instead, she says, "This is amazing." She looks so serious I wonder if she's pulling my leg. "You are a great writer,

Kate. And the ski mask idea is genius. I was wondering how you were going to make the switch."

"It's not bad," I say modestly. "I could have done better if I had more time."

"No, it's amazing," she insists, and I decide it's silly to argue. The more I think about it, the more jazzed I am about having such a quirky, offbeat ending.

Then, almost as if she's reading my mind, Margaret fixes her thick-rimmed gaze on me. "Tim Burton would love this ending. It's completely Tim Burtonesque."

"You think so?" I feel absurdly pleased at the thought of Tim Burton reading my script. After weeks of being called *Crapkate*, it's nice to hear my movie mentioned in the same breath as a famous Hollywood director. "It's probably not gruesome enough."

"No, he would LOVE it," Margaret says. "I'm totally serious. I can't wait to see the rest of the movie."

I turn and fiddle with my camera so she won't see my cheeks turning pink.

"I don't get it," Doris says. "Why is she wearing a winter coat and ski mask since it's not winter outside?"

"It's winter in my movie," I explain. "I shot some scenes with Alyssa last January, and I have a shot of her running up to the door in one of our big coats and a ski mask. I'll use that shot, then cut to a shot of Margaret coming inside with the same coat and mask on. The windows will blow out, so no one will see it isn't really winter outside."

Doris stares dubiously at me. "You're going to blow up your windows?"

"Blow out," I correct, "which means all you'll see is light. You won't see any details. So it could be winter or summer—you won't know."

Doris scratches her nose. "Then why is it summer when she goes outside at the end?"

"It's *symbolic*," Margaret answers. "The reign of the zombies is over. Like in *The Lion, the Witch and the Wardrobe*, the snow melts when the White Witch loses her power. Right?" she says, looking at me.

"Exactly." Actually, I made it summer because I don't have a huge snowmaking machine to make it look like winter, but I like Margaret's answer better.

Margaret gives a breathless laugh and then bites her lower lip. "I'm a little nervous."

"You'll be fine." I try to say it like I mean it, but I'm nervous, too. If Margaret is a horrible actress, then my movie will end on a big flat note. But part of a director's job is to keep her actors happy, so I smile brightly and say, "Okay, let's get started."

Derek walks in just then with his buddy, Trevor. They look bored, which means trouble.

"Who are the zombies?" Doris asks.

"You. And my brother, Derek, here and his friend."

Derek stares at Doris. "She looks like a zombie."

"Derek!" I have to sound really mad to keep myself from

smiling, because it's kind of true. With her sallow skin and stringy hair, Doris will need the least amount of makeup of any of my zombies.

Doris shrugs. "That's okay. Studies have shown that a lot of boys at this age are developmentally delayed, so their behavior patterns mimic younger children's."

Derek stares at her with his mouth open. "Huh?"

"She says you're acting like a five-year-old, but don't worry, it's normal. Now go away," I tell him. "I'll call you when your scene is up."

"We're bored," he whines. "Let us help. We'll do whatever you want."

I think about him watching my last shoot from the window, probably wishing he could be part of it. Life in the country isn't always much fun for Derek, either.

"Fine," I say. "You can help with props. Go get Mom's old winter coat, the big blue one, and I need a hard-boiled egg to put in the pocket. There are a few in the fridge."

Derek and Trevor run off, and it occurs to me that it's not so bad having a crew to order around.

Finally, we're ready to shoot the first scene. My camera is set up in the laundry room, pointed at the door. In the huge down coat and ski mask, Margaret could easily pass for Alyssa.

I give the cue, and Margaret runs inside and slams the door. She delivers her first lines perfectly. Usually, Alyssa flubs her lines the first few times. "This is the only food I found." Margaret pulls the egg from her pocket, right on cue. "If I eat this egg, I'll turn into a zombie. But I don't care anymore."

Margaret isn't a bad actress. She must really be feeling the moment and gripping the egg tightly because there's a sudden loud crack as it explodes, and goopy yolk spurts everywhere.

Derek and Trevor howl with laughter and run off. "You're fired!" I shout after them. "You can forget about being zombies!"

Just as Derek turns around to stick out his tongue, Margaret cocks her arm and flings the egg, a gloppy rocket that hits him square in the face. His mouth fills with raw yolk, and egg slime slides down his neck. Derek runs to the sink, screaming and gagging. Even though I'm the director, Margaret and Doris have to pick me up off the floor, I'm laughing so hard. We're definitely off to a good start.

"I should have known better than to let those two take care of props," I mutter later to Margaret as I wipe egg off my camera. "Where did you learn how to throw like that?"

Margaret shrugs modestly. "I have a little brother, too."

I grab a hard-boiled egg from the fridge, and the rest of the scene goes smoothly. When it's time to move downstairs, our moldy, cobwebby basement doesn't seem to faze Margaret and Doris at all. With them there, even the cistern doesn't seem nearly so scary.

I put Doris in charge of special effects, give her a glove,

and stick her on a stepladder. She quickly screws and unscrews the overhead lightbulb so it looks like the lights are flickering after Mallory eats the zombie egg. Then, I shake the camera just enough to make it look like an earthquake. When Margaret slowly peels off the ski mask, a shiver runs down my spine and a lump rises in my throat. This is the climax of all my hard work. My zombie movie has risen out of the ashes.

I'm forced to reinstate Derek and Trevor as zombies for lack of any other options. Once they're in wardrobe and make a bunch of zombie noises at each other, they finally calm down and do a good job stomping down the stairs. Doris is the head zombie.

"All hail the Zombie Queen," she says in her flat monotone. The funny thing is, it fits the zombie character perfectly, and the scene goes way better than I expected. At the end, Margaret gets caught up in the moment and even ad-libs a little. She takes a step up the stairs, then solemnly says, "Finally, I go from darkness into light, the light of a new and better day." Then she slowly climbs the stairs and disappears into the bright rectangle of the open doorway.

It's pure art.

As Margaret hurries back down the basement stairs, we all start clapping, even Derek and Trevor.

"I hope you don't mind," she says, blushing. "It just kind of came out. We can do it again if you want."

"It was perfect," I assure her. "I couldn't have written it better myself."

We head upstairs, where the sun is already starting to set. We grab the last shot of Mallory walking into the sunset. Sure, it's a little cliché, but it looks great. Another lump rises in my throat. My zombie movie is in the can, as the movie people say. This is the moment I've been waiting for. I get to shout the three sacred words of moviedom used by every director, big and small. The woods swell with birdsong, a cool breeze blows against my cheek, and Margaret's hair looks like it's caught fire in the late-afternoon light. I wonder if George Lucas felt this good when he finished *Star Wars*.

I fill my lungs with air and shout: "IT'S A WRAP!"

26

We mill around in the road for a while as I savor the wonderful feeling of finishing my movie. Then suddenly, I'm starving hungry. My mother makes a pizza and Margaret, Doris, and I sit on the back steps, laughing and talking. It feels good to be hanging out with friends. Margaret and Doris both seem excited about being in my film. It's definitely a big change from my last shoot with Alyssa and Lydia.

Margaret turns to me and says out of the blue: "I heard Paul Corbett got in big trouble a few days ago."

This doesn't surprise me. He's always in trouble. "What did he do this time?"

"Stealing. He got caught at the Quik-Hop Pit-Stop stealing a CD." Her big blue eyes turn on me. "Isn't that stupid?"

She seems to be waiting for a reply, so I nod. It feels like all the leaves around us have stopped moving, and my heart along with them. Is Margaret just making conversation, or is she making a point?

"He probably thought it was no big deal," Margaret says. I wish she would look away. I feel pinned under her bright blue gaze. "But now he has to go in front of a judge. And my mom says he'll probably have to do community service work."

"It will do him good," I mutter. I look away and fumble with my drink. Why does Margaret keep staring at me?

She looks down but an accusing silence remains. *She knows, she knows, she knows.* The words drum in my head. I can feel myself starting to sweat. Finally, I can't stand it any longer. "Just what are you trying to say?" I ask loudly.

Margaret gazes at me. Her eyes are a little too wide open, a little *too* surprised. "What do you mean?"

"You know what I mean." I feel like I'm choking on the words.

She gives me the same innocent look. "What would I be trying to say?"

"If you don't know, then I don't know, either," I mutter.

Doris is staring between us like we're both crazy. "What are you talking about?"

I feel like I'm suddenly in an old Donald Duck cartoon, with a tiny angel perched on one shoulder and a red devil on the other.

It will be a relief to tell someone, the angel whispers. *She already knows, anyway. It's time to come clean.*

Don't be stupid! the devil screams. *Keep it a secret! Cover your tracks!*

Yes, I need to keep it secret. It's funny, though, how a secret can feel so heavy. After a while, you just want to put it down and rest. I close my eyes and listen to the leaves murmuring in the trees. It sounds like they're saying *shush, shush, shush.* But I can't.

"I did it," I whisper.

Doris peers at me. "Did what?"

Then, just like that, my desire to confess is gone, replaced by icy-cold fear. I can't afford to lose the only two friends I have. I grab another piece of pizza. "Nothing," I say through a mouthful of cheese. "Just kidding."

It's the first time I've seen Doris look so confused. Margaret also takes a slice and nibbles on it. The way she's not looking at me, I know it's too late.

I nod, even though she hasn't asked.

"The wig?" Her voice is so quiet I almost don't hear it.

I keep nodding. My cheeks are burning and I wish I could sink into the dirt.

"The wig?" Doris echoes. "Are you talking about the red wig Alyssa took?"

I'm hoping Margaret will jump in and explain everything, but she just looks at me.

"I took it," I mutter. "It wasn't Alyssa."

"You?" Doris sounds surprised. "Why would you take it?"

I thought I would feel better getting it off my chest, but I only feel ashamed. My face burns as I explain my plan and I can hardly get the words out. I even explain about film noir and how the bad guys always take the fall, and how Alyssa was the bad guy. As I say it out loud, it all sounds pretty lame.

Margaret gazes down at her pizza when I get to the part about using her to get the note to Alyssa. "I wanted to teach her a valuable lesson," I say quickly. "I wanted her to know what it's like to get hurt by her friends, so she won't do it again to someone else."

Doris nods like she gets it. "You wanted revenge."

"No!" I wriggle in my seat. "Well, maybe a little. Can you blame me?"

Now even Margaret and Doris think badly of me. What if they don't want to sit with me anymore at lunch? It would be like a so-sad-it's-funny scene out of a movie—Alyssa and me eating our lunches in side-by-side bathroom stalls because no one else wants to sit with us.

Finally, Margaret speaks. I'm expecting she'll be mad, but her voice is quiet. "I get why you did it, after the way Alyssa treated you. It was really stupid, but I get it. But now I'm kind of part of it. You made me an accessory."

"No one would blame you," I quickly say. "Anyway, no one will know." I give them a sideways look. "I mean, unless you decide to tell someone."

Doris has been busy polishing her glasses, not looking at me. A few weeks ago, I was embarrassed to sit with her. Now I feel a horrible sinking in my stomach at the thought I've disappointed her. She finally glances at me. Her brown eyes are really sort of pretty now that I can actually see them. "That depends on what you're going to do."

"I was only going to hold on to the wig a couple of weeks and then return it," I say eagerly. "Once the wig is back, no one will care. No harm done."

"People will still think Alyssa took it," Margaret points out. "They'll always remember. Even in high school, she'll be the girl who stole the wig in seventh grade."

"And I'll still be remembered as Crapkate," I retort. "They're going to write in my yearbook: *The girl most likely to step in crap.*" My voice goes up a notch. "I only did to her what she did to me!"

Doris carefully replaces her glasses. She turns her newly cleaned focus on me. "Do you think it was Alyssa's fault that crap fell off your shoe?"

"Well, no. She made fun of me afterward, though. She ditched me to hang out with Lydia."

"So she made things worse, but she didn't cause the problem," Doris says slowly, like she's working out a logic problem. "She didn't set out to hurt you on purpose, correct?"

I'm not sure how to answer, so I just shrug.

"And she didn't try to get you in trouble at school, or with the other kids."

"No," I mutter. Doris has dissected the ugly matter like it was a dead frog in biology class. My shriveled black heart lies exposed for all the world to see. I know it's selfish to worry about myself, but I can't help asking again, "Are you guys going to tell anyone?"

Margaret and Doris glance at each other. My life hangs in the balance. They both shake their heads, and I breathe a huge sigh of relief.

"I think we should help you undo the mess, not make it worse," Margaret says. "We need to come up with a new plan."

27

Over the next few days, I think hard, but once again I come up blank. I have no idea how to return the wig and get Alyssa off the hook for taking it. I can only hope that Margaret's and Doris's supersize brains will hatch a plan. I'm so thankful they're not giving me the cold shoulder that I would gladly follow any scheme they come up with.

I also don't want to think about the baby monitor stuffed in my closet. After risking my life to rescue it from the basement, I can't find the nerve to use it. I'm scared of what I might hear. Plus, I'm not keen about adding *snoop* to my list of dubious achievements.

It's much easier to focus on my movie. I'm excited as I watch the final scene we shot. I've already edited parts of my movie, but now it's time to get serious about finishing it. I recently read on the Internet that making a movie longer than two hours is a serious no-no unless you're a big-name director with a megastar cast. Movie theaters can't show a long movie as many times per night, which means they make less money. It's all about pushing the popcorn and making a buck. I figure if the big boys can keep their blockbusters to two hours, then so can I. I have to grit my teeth as I slash scenes that took days of work to write, plan, and shoot. It feels a little like I'm slashing my own children.

It turns out I have way too many scenes of Alyssa being chased by zombies and not enough footage of the hens. At least, not good footage. Even though Alyssa and I tried to capture zombie behavior, in most shots the hens are running away from the camera.

If I had a big budget, I could call up one of those Hollywood animal companies and it'd ship me over some trained chickens, no problem. They probably have hens that will drop dead on command or run around in circles and act berserk. Or I could hire a special effects guy to make their eyes glow red and give them huge razor claws and beaks. But since I'm on a shoestring budget, it's all up to me. I've got to make those ladies perform.

I take my camera out to the chicken coop, watching the hens from the corner of my eye. In *Chicken Run*, the hens have a secret room underneath the chicken coop where they make all their plans. I jump up and down, testing the floorboards. They seem solid enough. I stroll over to their laying beds and dig under the straw. No hidden trap doors.

Suddenly, I feel silly. Of course there aren't any trap doors. That was an animated film about hens that built an airplane, blew up a barn, and flew the coop. These ladies clucking at my feet are real birds, simple barnyard animals. There's no plan to ruin my life. The only thing they know how to do is eat and peck and poop. They're all watching me right now, but only because they're used to me serving up their meals. They probably can't figure out why I'm not feeding them.

My camera is set up on its tripod in a corner of the coop. I turn it on, then take out a box of my mom's organic oatmeal. Hens love oatmeal. I grab two handfuls of it and fling them into the air. The hens go crazy, trying to snap up the flakes. I throw another handful and some of it lands on their backs, so now the hens are pecking at each other, too. They're not hurting each other—they just want the oatmeal—but in the camera it looks like a chicken mob scene. In my movie, this scene will come right after the hens have eaten the polluted chicken feed, when they're all starting to zombify.

After the oatmeal is gone, a hen I've named Spike wanders over and pecks at my tripod, like she's hoping it's a big black worm she can gobble up. Spike may not have lots of brains, but she's at the top of the pecking pyramid. She's a tough chick, with a mean beak and a quick claw. I'm surprised her eggs don't come out hard-boiled.

Spike tries to peck at my shoe, and I shove her away with my foot, but this gives me an idea. I've been trying to get a super close-up shot of just an eye and a beak, but whenever I get near a hen with my camera, she gets nervous and bolts. Spike seems pretty fearless; maybe she will let me get my shot.

I open the coop door and the hens bolt out after me.

I shake out some more oatmeal in the grass, then sink down at eye level near Spike and focus my camera. At first she gives me the evil eye, but she's distracted by the oatmeal. The shot would be better if her eyes were rolling backward and rabid foam dripped from her beak, but I can't get too picky. Just as I hit the on button, I hear the loud crunch of gravel behind me, and Derek shouts, "Whatcha doin'?"

Spike squawks and runs away. The rest of the birds scatter. Another great film moment lost forever. "Derek!" I shout. "You scared them off!"

"Sorry," he says, his voice whiny. "I just wanted to see what you were doing."

Sometimes I think Spike has a bigger IQ than Derek. "When I'm pointing my camera at something and looking through the viewfinder, that means I'm shooting video."

I say it sarcastically, but he just nods and kicks at the grass. Then he grins sideways at me. "Wanna see something funny?"

"No."

"Come on," he whines. "It's really funny."

"Fine, whatever. Just hurry up."

I'm thinking he's got something stupid in his pocket to show me, but he reaches up and sticks his finger in his nose and starts shoveling around inside.

"That is not funny," I inform him. "That is totally lame."

"Just wait." He's actually biting his tongue in concentration as he fishes around. I watch him, horrified. How will I ever win back friends with a little brother like this?

Derek finally pulls out his finger and shows me his disgusting prize. Then he leans over and offers it to a nearby hen. She cranes her neck forward. It probably looks like squished worm guts. She nervously dances around, then darts over and gobbles it off his finger. Derek grins at me like he's just taught the bird to speak French.

I'm so revolted I don't even know what to say. But I can't help it; the corner of my mouth twitches. The thought of my mother's elite hens eating Derek's nose snot is kind of funny.

Derek lets out a hoot. "Trevor and I must have fed them half a pound yesterday. They love it!"

"You are so weird," I murmur. "You're lucky Mom didn't catch you."

"Yeah, she'd be like"—he scrunches up his face and makes his voice screechy—"'Derek, those boogers aren't certified organic. What are you thinking?'"

At this, I break out laughing and Derek grins.

"What are you doing?" he asks again. "Can I help?"

"Ha. Like you helped last time with the egg in the pocket? I don't think so."

"Aw, come on, that was just a joke. I promise, I'll do whatever you say." He looks at me, jiggling up and down like's he's cold, even though it's perfectly warm out. "Come on, ple-e-ease? Pretty please? I'll get the chickens to do whatever you want. Please please please please..."

"Fine!" I tell him, just to shut him up. I sigh loudly but secretly I'm glad. It's more fun shooting with someone else.

As Derek helps me herd the hens, it reminds me of when we were younger. He and I used to spend hours playing together with our toys. We loved to pretend that his trolls were slaves in my Barbie castle. They had to brush the Barbies' hair, cook their meals, and wash their dresses, all because of a curse laid on them by the evil Transformer space aliens. In the last couple of years, we've done more fighting than playing. Maybe fighting is the only thing we know how to do together anymore, now that I'm too old to play with toys.

"So what kind of shots do you want?" Derek asks, suddenly all business.

"I'd love to get a hen flying at the camera like it's attacking, but it's impossible. I've tried sprinkling oatmeal near the lens, and insects...."

Derek snaps his fingers like, no big deal. "I'll throw one at the camera. It'll look like it's attacking."

"Derek!" I may not like the chickens, but I can't believe he wants to throw one. "Mom would kill us."

"A little toss doesn't hurt them," he scoffs. "They have wings. They land on their feet."

"You mean you've done this before?"

He grins. "Trevor and I had a contest once to see which hen would fly the farthest."

"Who won?"

"Henrietta. She went about half a mile trying to get away from us!"

Derek runs after Henrietta, as if to show me. She tries to scurry away, but he catches her like an old pro. I'm impressed despite myself. I tried to pick up Spike once, and she gave me a nasty peck on the hand. Since then, I've avoided trying to grab the ladies.

Derek carries Henrietta inside the coop, where our mother can't see us. I set my camera at a low angle in a corner, and he stands just out of frame. When I give him the cue, he gives Henrietta a gentle toss. Sure enough, she flaps her wings like crazy and lands right in front of the lens. She skids a little, kicking up dust, then squawks and bolts away.

"That was perfect!" I shout.

Derek grins modestly. It occurs to me that I should have hired him a lot earlier. I never would have gotten that shot with Alyssa. She's even more scared than I am to touch the chickens.

We spend the rest of the afternoon shooting together.

Derek even grabs Spike and holds her tight so I can finally zoom in and get my crazed eyeball shot.

I'd forgotten how much fun my little brother can be. I even let Derek hold my camera and get a few shots on his own. When we're done, he hands the camera back to me.

"You know, I think I'm going to make a movie, too," he says.

On another day this might have made me mad, because he's always copying what I do. But I realize it's probably the biggest compliment Derek can pay me. It's like he's saying that he wants to be like me.

So I clap him on the shoulder. "Just do yourself a favor. DON'T make a movie about chickens."

"Nah," he says. "Mine's going to be about vampires."

"Good choice."

He grins sideways at me. "Race you to the house?"

I roll my eyes. "We're not six anymore."

He looks down and I'm gone, camera and all, feet pounding as fast as I can. It feels good to run, to hear him hooting and hollering behind me, to laugh as we collapse on the porch steps together. Most of all, it feels good to get there a step ahead of Derek. It won't be too many years before he will suddenly be taller than I am, with a deep voice rumble I won't even recognize. I know, because I already see the boys at school changing. At least for now, though, Derek still looks up to me. At least for now, I'm still faster than my little squirt brother.

28

It's funny, but I've been noticing that hardly anyone calls me *Crapkate* anymore. In fact, my old friends run up to me in the hallway; they all want to talk about Alyssa. I shrug. It feels like I'm in the wrong movie. I should be all happy, but I'm not. I can't just forget about all the weeks where they ignored me. We talk and it's nice, but it's definitely not back to normal. I still sit with Margaret and Doris at lunch.

Luckily, no one sits close by, because our conversation is all about Alyssa and the wig.

"I was thinking about... what we talked about on Saturday," Margaret tells me. "I think I have an idea how to return the item in question."

I feel a cold jolt in my stomach. I'd been focusing on my movie, trying to forget about that item.

Doris leans forward. "Good, let's hear it."

"First, I watched *The Maltese Falcon* yesterday. Just to see what you were talking about, Kate. You're right, great movie. And I did some research on film noir on the Internet. To try to get some ideas."

I can only listen, amazed. If this were a school project, Margaret would get an A-plus. I'm guessing that's an average grade for her.

"So anyway," she goes on, "I asked myself, what would Bogie do? What would the Beautiful Dame do? And it hit me. What does every film noir tough guy have? An airtight alibi!" She beams at us, then modestly adds, "Well, that's what I read on the Internet, anyway."

"You're incredible, Margaret," I tell her.

She blushes pink. It occurs to me that Margaret probably doesn't get a lot of compliments.

Doris nods thoughtfully. "You're right. Alyssa needs an alibi."

"I thought we could do it during choir class," Margaret goes on. "I'll stick my head into the music room on the way to class and make a comment to someone about how the wig is still missing. Alyssa can get sick and leave class early. Then Kate can put the wig back, and we'll make sure someone discovers it."

Right away, I notice one huge flaw in the plan.

"We would have to tell Alyssa so she would know to leave early," I point out.

Margaret sips her drink, not looking at me. "Don't you think maybe you should tell her? Doesn't she kind of deserve to know?"

Now they're both gazing at me.

"No," I say right away. "No. I can't tell her. She doesn't know I took it, and she doesn't need to know I'm putting it back. As long as I get her off the hook, that's what matters."

My voice must sound a little mad, or desperate maybe, because Margaret quickly says, "Okay, okay." She plays with the straw in her drink. I can tell she's not happy with my answer, but there's no way I'm telling Alyssa, period.

Doris clears her throat. "There's another problem with that idea. Everyone would think Alyssa put the wig back after she left class early. They would still think she did it."

I sigh with relief. Off the hook.

Margaret frowns. "Yeah, you're right. But when else can we do it? First, people need to see that the wig is missing. Then, after Alyssa's alibi is in place, they need to see the wig has been returned. That way, they'll know Alyssa couldn't have done it."

"I don't know," I say gloomily. "But *Annie* auditions are Monday. I need to get this wig back quick."

Doris stares at me.

"What?" I wipe my mouth, thinking I must have left a blob of jelly.

Doris does her cackle-honk laugh. "That's it."

"Of course!" Margaret cries.

I'm definitely out of my IQ league here. "Of course what?"

Doris pushes her glasses up her nose like she does when I don't get a math problem. "Return it during auditions."

I snort. "Auditions?" I can't think of a worse time to try to pull it off.

"No, listen, it'll work," Doris says. "After Alyssa auditions, she'll leave, right? She's not going to want to hang around. Once she's gone, you and Margaret make sure people see the wig is still missing. You wait a little while, Kate, and then you slip in and return the wig. After that, you just have to make sure someone sees it's back. Alyssa will already be gone. Everyone will realize that she couldn't have done it."

Margaret's curls bounce as she nods. "I think it can work."

I'm already shaking my head. "People will get suspicious if I'm just hanging around during auditions. I mean, why would I be there?"

Doris and Margaret exchange a look.

"No way," I say. "NOT happening."

"It's the only way," Doris says.

"It'll be fun," Margaret insists.

"It will be a disaster," I groan.

If I'm going to be at the auditions to restore the Cute Red Wig, then I need a good reason to be there. My stomach flutters nervously at the thought. This is surely my punishment for taking the wig. In order to return it and make things right, I will have to audition for a role in *Annie*.

We spend the rest of the week talking over the plan, making sure we've thought of everything. I know exactly what I need to do on Monday. Then, on Saturday, everything changes.

29

I'm in my pajamas, watching Saturday morning cartoons and eating a bowl of cereal. I'm totally relaxed, knowing I have the whole day free in front of me to do whatever I want. Then my mom walks in and hands me an envelope. I recognize the handwriting right away. I rip it open and there's a hand-drawn card—a sad face with tears leaking out of the eyes. It won't win any art prizes, but I get the point. I'm so shocked I have to turn off the TV. This is the last thing I expected. I'm even more surprised when, a couple of hours later, my cell phone rings. I'm tempted to ignore it, but I have to know why she's calling.

"Hi."

Silence. The caller takes a deep breath and I hear a catch. "I'm such a jerk."

I stare at my fingernails and try to keep my voice light. "Yeah, kind of."

"I'm sorry, Kate. I know you're mad at me. I don't blame you, but I just wanted to let you know. I'm really sorry."

"You're sorry now that everyone at school hates you," I point out. "Now that you're not Lydia's best friend anymore."

"I never wanted to be her best friend." Alyssa hesitates. "At first, we had a lot to talk about. You know, with her parents getting divorced and everything. But we weren't getting along very well at the end. Like, nothing I said was funny anymore, but I was still supposed to laugh at all her stupid jokes. She was hanging with Tina Turlick most of the time."

Sure, Alyssa wants to be friends now, I tell myself. She comes running back because Lydia's dumped her. Everyone hates her. Her social life is in shreds. So who does she call? Crapkate Walden. I'm her last resort, her fallback, her Plan Z.

"So why are you telling all this to me? I'm just a loser, remember? The weirdo with chicken crap on her shoes."

There's a silence. For a second, I think maybe she hung up. "I don't blame you for hating me," Alyssa finally says. "But you're not a loser. You're a ten times better friend than Lydia."

For a moment, I feel better because I know it's true. Then a horrible feeling comes over me as I realize it's *not* true.

"I knew I was being stupid, but I just couldn't help

myself," Alyssa says, real quiet. "It's like I was on drugs or something. All the girls crowding around, and suddenly everything I said was superfunny, and everyone wished they were me...."

"Not everyone," I say loudly.

I hear a tiny sniff and I know she's crying.

"I've got to go," I say quickly. I hang up, not waiting for her to answer.

My head is whirling. In the little movie that's been running in my brain, this is the part where I get superexcited. I've watched the rerun in my head so many times it's starting to show up in my dreams at night. It's the one where Alyssa admits she's all wrong and I beam happily as she begs my forgiveness.

Now it's happening and I don't feel superexcited. When I check the mirror, I'm not beaming. Mostly, I feel confused. Part of me wants my BFF back. I want life to go back to normal. But things aren't the same. I'm not sure I'm the same. I have other friends now and there's no way I'm going to turn around and ignore Margaret and Doris. I know how bad it feels.

I saw girls who were best buddies in grade school turn into strangers once they hit junior high. Usually, one of the girls changed a lot over the summer while the other didn't change at all. Suddenly, they had nothing in common. Is that what's happened to Alyssa and me? Are we just two different people now? Or was the last month just a temporary insanity? Has Alyssa really come to her senses, or will she dump me again once things blow over? I couldn't go through all this again. I'm afraid my heart might explode.

Still, Alyssa was my friend for six years. Should I let a few bad weeks ruin all those years of friendship? What if Lydia had gotten chummy with me instead? I might have acted the same way. I might have drunk the Lydia Kool-Aid and let it go to my head.

My relaxed feeling is gone. Instead, I'm chewing one fingernail after another, trying to figure out what to do. Finally, I send a text. *We should talk. Come over tomorrow?*

Right away, she calls. "You mean it?"

"Sure," I say gruffly. "We can talk about what a lousy friend you've been and how you're going to make it up to me."

"I *was* a sucky friend. But you know, Hitch," Alyssa says, real solemn, "I didn't take the Cute Red Wig. It wasn't me."

"I know," I say.

I hear her voice catch. "You mean it? You really believe me?"

The Cute Red Wig is hidden in a box inside a bag at the back of my closet under a stack of old shoes. Still, I feel like it's sending out some kind of weird signal that Alyssa will be able to hear, like a foghorn blast or a time bomb ticking.

"Of course I believe you," I say.

Alyssa starts telling me how great I am and what a super friend I am. Every time she says something I feel a little worse. Something starts rising up inside me, like a balloon filling with helium. Only it's not helium. It's a strange gas called guilt and it's building in my throat and choking me. I'm the one who should be apologizing to her. "I gotta go," I finally blurt. "I'll see you tomorrow."

I pace back and forth in my room. More than ever, I wish I could rewind the past couple of weeks and cut out some crucial scenes. My plan didn't seem so terrible at the time. We were all just actors playing a part. But life is turning out to be way more complicated than any movie. In film noir, the bad guy always takes the fall. All along, I thought Alyssa was the bad guy. Life has added one last twist, though. Now it turns out the bad guy might be me.

I stare at myself in the mirror. The narrow rectangle of glass looks like a tiny jail and I'm trapped inside it. If life really were a movie, then I'd be in handcuffs by now, headed to prison for stealing, forgery, lying, and general all-around bad-guy behavior. I deserve to have the cops kick in my door and lock me up in the slammer. I imagine myself holding on to the bars of my cell as the camera dollies backward to reveal a long, echoing prison hallway, with me at the very end, lost in shadow. . . .

Okay, maybe I've watched a few too many film noir movies.

Still, the person in the mirror seems like a stranger. I always thought the idea of turning into somebody else was just a cute Hollywood plot gimmick, like in *Freaky Friday*.

It feels like that's what's happened to me, though, minus the body exchange. How did I turn into this mean, vengeful thief?

I wander over to my window and stare outside. Maybe I should have just called Alyssa and talked to her instead of getting so upset. Maybe I should have accepted that people do change. I certainly have.

I pull out my phone and text Margaret: *Heard from A. We're talking tomorrow.*

Immediately, she texts back. *Wow! Good luck. Going to tell her?*

I think about this for a long time. Finally, I write: *idk.* It's probably not the answer she wants to hear, but it's the best I've got.

After texting with Margaret, I keep pacing back and forth in my room, going over what I should say and do when she comes over. I feel an overwhelming urge to talk to my mother. I figure she's probably busy counting her chickens or something, but when I walk downstairs she's sitting at the kitchen table, rubbing her temples. She looks worried and I suddenly feel funny barging in on her. It looks like she doesn't need yet another headache. I'm just about to back out the door when she glances up and smiles at me.

"Hi, honey."

"Hi." I sit down, wondering why she looks so tired. "Is something wrong?"

She hesitates, then shrugs. "I lost my biggest restaurant client today. They're closing their doors."

"Burberry's is closing?"

She nods. "And the sales figures for last month aren't what I'd hoped. And some of the hens have a fungal infection—" She shoots a quick glance at me and smiles. "Sorry. I promise, no medical details."

"It's okay. You can talk about that stuff. I overreacted."

My mother shakes her head. "No, you were right. I've been so busy trying to make this business work I got too caught up in it. I forgot I have a more important job."

I'm confused. "Another job?"

"Being a mom." She smiles ruefully. "You know, Kate, I always wished I could live on a farm when I was your age. I loved animals, but your grandmother was allergic to everything. The only pet I ever had was a fish. I wanted to give you and Derek a chance to enjoy all the things I missed." She glances wistfully around the kitchen. "I guess one person's dream is another's nightmare. I've dragged you both out into the country, away from everything. And now you have these problems with your friends." She gives a deep sigh. "I'm starting to think this was all a big mistake."

I'm tempted to agree with her. It's on the tip of my tongue to blurt *Does that mean we can lose the chickens and move back to town?*

But I bite back the thought. The sadness in her face reminds me of how I felt when I thought I had to give up on my movie. When I lost my best friend. It's true that my mother's heavenly hens have turned out to be devils in disguise. Instead of a movie about zombie chickens, I should have made a flick about gangster hens, hatching eggs by day and criminal plots by night. On the other hand, Alyssa and I had a lot of fun chasing after them. Hens aren't the easiest animal in the world to direct, but some of our biggest laughs came from trying.

It's nice to hear that she still thinks being our mom is an important job. It's nice that she's worried about me. Maybe the hens haven't won her over to the dark side yet. Maybe my mom doesn't hate me as much as I thought. Maybe she doesn't even hate me at all.

"Without the hens I wouldn't have my movie," I point out. "And you'd still be stuck at a job you didn't like."

And then it hits me—my mother and I are trying to do the same thing. We've gotten on each other's nerves and we've gotten in each other's way. We've both run into roadblocks. But all this time, we've both been trying to follow our passion. Okay, hers is a little weird, but some people could say the same about making a movie.

Instead of backing her up, I've spent all my energy hating her new business and complaining about it. Now she's thinking about calling it quits, and I might be partly to blame. I guess I have to add *being a bad daughter* to my list of accomplishments. I'm glad the day is almost over. I don't think I can stand to find too many more character defects.

I remember how excited my mother was when she announced her new business to us and lit her old clothes on fire. It hurts when you have a dream and it gets squashed. I've learned all about that. So I take a deep breath.

"You can't quit now, Mom. Derek and I are surviving just fine. This is your dream. You have to go for it. If you don't do it now, when will you ever do it? You and Dad aren't getting any younger."

My mother mock frowns at me. "Are you calling me old?"

I shrug. "I'm just saying."

She looks me right in the eye. "Are you sure, Kate?"

For a second, I have a flicker of doubt. This is my chance to get rid of those hens once and for all. If I'm lucky, Spike might end up in a can of chicken soup. . . .

I meet her gaze. "I'm sure."

She gives me a relieved smile. "Don't worry, I'm not throwing in the towel yet. But thanks for the pep talk. I definitely needed to hear that." She gives me a searching look. "Now, how about you? How's your movie coming along?"

"It's okay." I nervously fidget with a lock of hair. Now that I'm sitting in front of her, I'm not sure what to say.

She gives me one of her concerned-mom looks. "Anything wrong?"

A lump rises in my throat as I nod. Then, it all comes spilling out. Sort of. "I have these two friends and they had a fight. One friend . . . borrowed something. The other friend doesn't know about it, but she ended up getting in trouble because of it." I avoid her gaze. I know I'm not fooling her with the two-friends bit.

My mother nods thoughtfully. "Did your friend ask before borrowing the item?"

I shake my head. I can feel my cheeks reddening.

"Then that's a little like stealing," my mother says gently. "I would advise the borrower to return the item and then tell her friend what she did."

"What if she tells her friend and then the friend hates her forever?"

My mother takes my hand and squeezes it. "It's hard to do the right thing." She gazes at my fingernails, which are nibbled down to nubs, and for a moment I think she's going to lecture me. Instead, she gives my hand another squeeze. "You know, Kate, all of us get busy building our careers, building our families, our friendships. It's easy to forget that we're also building who we are. We do it every day. It's not what other people think of us that defines us. It's what we do and how we act. I guess your friend has to decide what kind of person she wants to be."

I nod. I expected my mother to freak out and demand to know what got stolen and how I'm involved. Instead, she leans over, strokes my hair, and asks if I want a cookie.

It reminds me of when I was young, when a kiss from

her along with a homemade chocolate chip cookie used to cure just about anything. I'm twelve now, though. Does my mother really think a cookie can help?

"I'm not hungry," I tell her. She kisses my forehead as she gets up to go, leaving me to ponder the horrible person I've become.

"Are they chocolate chip?" I ask, just out of curiosity.

Because even though a cookie won't help, I decide it won't hurt, either.

31

When Alyssa shows up at our door Sunday afternoon, my mother practically screams with excitement. She's so happy that I realize she must have been a lot more worried about our fight than she let on.

"It's so nice to see you again," she gushes. "I think you've grown since the last time you were here. How's your mom? Would you like a snack?"

It's kind of embarrassing, but it's also kind of sweet. Finally I rescue Alyssa and we escape upstairs. Then we're standing alone in my room, looking everywhere except at each other. Alyssa starts in and says she's sorry again. She's playing with the stuff on my dresser, but she suddenly turns toward me. "Hitch, I really didn't take the wig. Everyone thinks I did, but I didn't." She hesitates. "I was in the music room to meet Jake Knowles. He sent me a note, but then he didn't show up."

If it were me, I would have walked right up to Jake and asked him why he stood me up. But then again, I don't have a crush on him. Alyssa gets tongue-tied whenever she's near Jake, so I guess that's why she hasn't asked him.

I can feel the guilt balloon rising up inside me again. I know I should tell Alyssa. It's the right thing to do. Still, part of my brain is screaming, *Don't do it!* I think about what my mother said and I take a deep breath. And another. Then a few more.

"I know about Jake," I finally tell her.

She looks surprised. "Did he tell you?"

The balloon is huge. It's pressing against my chest. If I tell Alyssa, I'll be in a boatload of trouble. When she tells everyone what really happened, they will hate me. Mr. Cantrell will hate me. My classmates will think I'm a lying, stealing, two-faced, scheming loser. My parents will probably disown me. I think of Margaret and sigh. I know she would do the right thing.

Finally, the balloon in my chest pops. I cover my face with my hands. "I know because I did it!"

Alyssa looks worried. "Did what?"

I can't utter the words. I walk to my closet, dig down, and pull out the plastic bag. I have to move the baby monitor out of the way to reach it. Just seeing the monitor sends a nervous jolt through my body. I'd almost forgotten about my plan to spy on my dad. Is there no low deed I'm not capable of?

I grab the plastic bag, dump out the box, open it, and pull out the Cute Red Wig.

Alyssa gasps. Her eyes go round. A small, twisted part of me wishes I was getting all this on camera. I could use that reaction shot in my movie.

"You took it?" Alyssa shakes her head, looking confused. "Why?"

I tell her the whole terrible story. She gets mad—really mad—when I explain how I wrote the note, used Margaret to deliver it, and made sure Mr. Cantrell was in the hallway to see her.

"Wow, that is so low, I can't even... I can't believe you would..."

"You dumped me for Lydia!" I blurt. "You made my family sound moronic. And you were pathetic, making fun of Margaret. She didn't deserve that."

"But you did this on purpose," Alyssa says, her voice shaking. "You set the whole thing up for me to get in trouble. And now everyone hates me."

She glares at me and I wonder if she might even call the cops. Technically, I'm in possession of stolen property. Alyssa stalks to the door, then turns. Her lower lip trembles. "You have no idea how awful the last weeks have been."

"Yes, I do," I say quietly.

She pauses at my words and a funny look comes over her face. Then she slams shut the door. Just as I feared, she's never going to forgive me.

I hear my mother's voice on the landing. "You're not leaving already, are you, Alyssa?"

"Yeah, I have to go, Mrs. Walden." I can tell Alyssa is making a huge effort to behave normally. There's an unwritten law among us that you only act bad in front of your own parents. In front of other parents, you must always be a perfect angel.

"That's too bad." My mother's voice sounds tentative. "Kate has really missed you these last couple of weeks."

I grind my teeth. Trust my mother to say something completely embarrassing. I wait for Alyssa to say something like, *Yeah, she missed me so much she got me accused of stealing and turned the whole school against me.*

When she does finally answer, her voice is quiet. "Um, yeah, I missed her, too."

"Look what I found," my mother goes on. "I was cleaning out some old drawers and I found this birthday card you made for Kate on her seventh birthday. Isn't it adorable?"

I know the card. It's a cutout of a pink bunny with big ears and pipe cleaners glued on for whiskers. Alyssa wrote a crooked *Happy* on one ear and *Birthday* on the other and across the bunny's belly she scrawled my name with three hearts after it. Most of the pipe cleaners have fallen off. Okay, I'm a little mushy. I like to keep old mementos.

I've got my ear glued to the door. "She kept that?" Alyssa sounds surprised.

I hear my mother laugh and murmur something, then go into her bedroom. Alyssa stomps down the stairs and a moment later the front door slams.

I sink down on the bed, still clutching the wig, feeling sad and numb. It takes five minutes at least before the thought hits me—Alyssa doesn't have a ride home. Her mother isn't coming back for another couple of hours. Could she have started walking home? More likely, she called her mother and is waiting outside for her.

I move to the window, but Alyssa isn't on the front porch or near the garage. I move to my other window and there she is, sitting under a tree in our backyard. She's stuck here when she probably wants to be a million miles away. As I'm trying to decide what to do, she stands up and brushes the grass off her legs. Maybe she's going to walk home after all. It has to be fifteen miles, at least. She must really want to get away from me.

Alyssa walks to the front and stands in the driveway, kicking at gravel. She turns suddenly, but instead of walking toward the road, she comes inside the house. I have my ear glued to my bedroom door, trying to figure out what she's doing. I can't hear a thing. Then the stairs creak. Someone is definitely coming up the stairs. I jump away like the door is white hot, land on my bed, and scoop up a magazine. No, that looks stupid. I run to my desk, but my computer is off, so why would I be sitting at my desk? There's no time to turn it on, so I veer off and end up inside my closet. I've been meaning to clean it out for months. Okay, for about a year. Now would be a good time to start. I hold my breath, listening.

I know I heard Alyssa come upstairs. Every step has a different squeak, so it's impossible to sneak up on anyone. A few seconds pass and I don't hear anything. Is she outside my door, listening? Is she trying to think of some really cutting last words? Is she dialing the police on her cell phone? The door slowly opens. I brace myself for the worst.

Alyssa's eyes are glued to the floor. She clears her throat. "I think what you did really sucks." She stops and kicks at the carpet, then finally glances up at me. "But what I did was pretty mean, too. I guess that makes us even."

A huge weight rises off my chest. I nod, not sure what to say. Actually, I do know what to say, but it's amazing how hard it can be to utter two little words. If I don't say them right now, I might never get them out. I take a deep breath. "I'm sorry."

"Me, too."

We smile, not quite looking at each other. What do you say after *sorry*? I rack my brain. The silence stretches between us. Then Alyssa's mouth twists. She covers it with her hand but I can see it. She's grinning, and then she's giggling. I'm so relieved I start to laugh, too, and pretty soon we're breathless from nervous, happy laughter.

"It's kind of funny," Alyssa gasps.

I shake my head. "It's horrible. It's twisted."

"Yeah. Definitely twisted. But I kind of deserved it, I guess."

"Only a little." I'm still not sure if she's going to tell everyone or not.

Alyssa turns to face me. "You can just put back the wig. No one needs to know what happened. I'll help you."

"We thought about that, but then everyone will still think you took it."

Alyssa raises her eyebrows. "We?"

"Margaret and Doris."

"Margaret Dorkel?" she says slowly. "And Doris Drabburn? Are you serious?"

In the past, I would have giggled at the silly names, but now I just feel sad. "We came up with a plan. I mean, they didn't know about the first plan," I say quickly. "I told them afterward. They were upset, you know, that I did that. But they offered to help fix things. And we have a new plan."

I quickly explain our strategy, but Alyssa shakes her head. "Are you crazy? I'm not trying out."

This takes me by surprise. I thought she couldn't wait to audition. "It's our best chance. After your turn, you can go straight home. We'll make sure someone sees the wig is still missing. Then I'll slip in, put it back, and make sure it gets noticed. Once the Cute Red Wig is returned, everyone will figure it was just some weird practical joke. No one will care who took it." I only hope this is true.

"I'm NOT trying out," Alyssa repeats. "Everyone will stare at me and make nasty comments."

I sigh. "You can wait in the library. I'll text you right before your turn comes up. You can just hurry in, audition, and leave."

Alyssa is quiet a moment. "We could just tell everyone what happened."

"We could." I stare at my hands. I know this will be the social kiss of death for me, but it's Alyssa's call. She has the right to prove to everyone that she isn't the thief. Home-schooling is starting to sound like a definite option.

I can feel Alyssa's gaze on me. "Forget it, bad idea," she says. "I'll audition."

I breathe a huge sigh of relief even as I realize that, once again, Margaret was right. I needed to tell Alyssa. It was the right thing to do. Plus, it would have been a disaster Monday afternoon when she didn't show up for auditions. So the plan is back on track. It's not ideal—it will require perfect timing and a lot of luck, but right now it's the only plan we've got.

32

I'm not usually allowed to have sleepovers on school nights, but my mother agrees to let Alyssa sleep over that night when I tell her we're trying out for *Annie* the next day and we want to practice our lines. She's so thrilled that Alyssa and I are friends again that she says yes before I even get the question out.

Alyssa and I watch a movie, just to kill some time, and then we take Wilma outside and throw the tennis ball for her. As Alyssa is wrestling the ball from Wilma, she suddenly glances sideways at me. "So have you come up with an ending for *Night of the Zombie Chickens* yet? I was thinking we should try to finish it before it turns cold."

My face must look shocked because she laughs. "Don't tell me you deleted the whole thing."

I'd forgotten that Alyssa doesn't know about Margaret. I stammer, trying to think how to explain it. "Uh, well, you know, I figured you weren't going to want to work on it anymore."

Alyssa lifts an eyebrow. "You really did delete it?"

"Of course not!" I feel my face flush. "The thing is, I asked Margaret to help me finish it. And Doris."

Alyssa's mouth drops open. "Are you serious?"

"We've been hanging out together the last month," I remind her, "while you were hanging out with Lydia." I let this sink in, then I take a deep breath. "They're not so bad. I think you'd like them."

"Maybe." Alyssa shrugs. I can tell she isn't convinced. "So how did you finish the movie?"

I have no choice but to tell her. I explain how Mallory eats the zombie egg and transforms. "It's brilliant, isn't it?"

Alyssa wrinkles her nose. "Brilliant? Hitch, I'm Mallory. That's my part. I've been playing her for a year. And now you want me . . . Mallory . . . to turn into *Margaret*?"

"You were busy, remember?" I remind her. "You dumped me, remember? What was I supposed to do?"

Wilma's eyes are glued on the ball in Alyssa's hand. She's trembling from watching it so hard. She whines, jumps in the air, turns in circles. Alyssa cocks back her arm, and Wilma is off like a shot, her tiny legs churning.

Alyssa pauses, her arm still cocked back. "I know: why don't we just reshoot? It's not like you have to keep that ending, right? It sounds kind of weird, anyway. Write a new ending and we'll finish it."

Wilma runs back, panting, giving us the evil eye. I grab the ball from Alyssa and throw it. It seems strange to be thinking about the ending to my movie again. It felt good knowing it was done. Plus, I did shout *"It's a wrap!"* so that kind of makes it official. Still, there's a certain logic to Alyssa's words.

It *is* a little strange to have Mallory change into a new person at the very end of the movie. If I reshoot with Alyssa, *Night of the Zombie Chickens* will flow better. Plus, Alyssa and I are a little unsure around each other after everything that's happened. I don't want to do anything to make our friendship shakier.

A guilty pang shoots through me. Margaret is super-excited to be in my movie. Even Doris still asks me how the editing is coming along. Still, I'm the director. It's my job to make the tough decisions. Sometimes, the best scenes end up on the cutting room floor because they just don't fit. But would I really be cutting it for the right reason?

Wilma returns the ball and spits it at my feet. I scratch her behind the ears. The last time I threw the ball for her, I ended up with chicken crap on my shoe. I peek at the soles of my shoes, just to be sure. Clean.

It's funny how a little piece of poop can do so much damage. The memory of *Crapkate Walden* rings in my ears. I'm happy Alyssa and I are friends again, but I don't know if I completely trust her yet. Trust is kind of like an egg—it's easily broken. And once you've spilled it, you have a big mess on your hands.

I throw the ball and watch Wilma gallop after it. I can feel Alyssa's eyes on me, so I nod to her. "Okay. Let me think about it."

33

That night, I wake up to the sound of pouring rain and crackling thunder. Lightning bathes my room in an eerie glow. It seems like an omen. Alyssa and I have gone through the plan over and over. We both know what we have to do. Still, I have to stop myself from waking her up and quizzing her.

I've already bagged the wig and stashed it in my backpack. Now, in the middle of the night, that suddenly seems like a bad idea. I know my mother has already heard via the mom grapevine that the wig was stolen. What if she finds some reason to dig around in my backpack in the morning? What if my dad knocks the pack off the kitchen counter as he's rushing out the door to work? I can already see the slow-motion fall to the floor, the wig spilling out, the horrified reaction shots from my parents. These things happen all the time in movies. I decide that, first thing in the morning, I will stow my backpack safely in the car.

It takes me a long time to fall back asleep. Then, it seems like two seconds and it's morning. Sunshine pours through the window. It's exactly the kind of weather I'd hoped for—a blue-skies, everything's-going-my-way kind of day.

As soon as I'm dressed, I lug my backpack safely to the car. When I get back inside, Alyssa is still in bed. She's staring at the ceiling, the covers pulled up to her chin. "I'm nervous, Hitch."

"All you have to do is sing," I assure her. "I'll take care of the rest."

"That's what I'm afraid of."

"Hey, my last plan worked pretty well."

Alyssa gives me a look. "Yeah, a little too well."

"Margaret's going to help," I tell her, but she doesn't look reassured.

At breakfast, neither of us eats much. My dad folds up his newspaper and downs the rest of his coffee. "So, this is the big day. You girls nervous?"

Alyssa and I freeze. Then I realize he's talking about the auditions. "Yeah, a little bit."

"Don't be shy," my mother advises. "Just get up there and sing loud. Teachers like it when you sing loud."

Derek smirks. "He won't like it when Kate sings loud. She sounds like a dying walrus."

That's the funny thing about little brothers. They can be totally sweet one moment and a real pain in the butt the next. I decide it's time to teach him a lesson in manners. I push back my chair from the table and screw up my face like I'm about to cry.

"He's right," I moan. "I'm not trying out. Forget it!" I cover my face with my hands and then watch through my fingers as my mother gives Derek the evil eye.

"Since you're so concerned with Kate's audition, Derek, you can feed the hens for her this morning. And clean out the coop after school today."

Derek's mouth drops open in horror. "Clean the coop! All I said was—"

"We heard what you said," my father sternly interrupts. "Kate has a beautiful voice."

I open my hands enough to lift an eyebrow and smirk at Derek. *That will teach you to mess with me.*

"She's making a face at me—" Derek whines.

"That's enough!" My mother slaps down her spatula and Derek knows better than to say another word. "Don't listen to your brother, Kate," my mother says in a softer voice. "You'll do just fine."

It's a great feeling to have my mother backing me up. I quirk another eyebrow at Derek. He doesn't take the bait, but his face turns red from the effort of holding it in. His eyes narrow and he lifts his chin. *Just wait. Your payback is going to suck.*

I bat my eyelids. *So scared*.

Derek shoves back from the table and stomps outside. Alyssa smirks. My parents haven't noticed a thing, of course.

Alyssa and I go to my bedroom to finish getting ready. Just as I predicted, the day is getting off to a great start. Seeing Derek get his just reward makes me feel giddy. Or maybe it's nerves.

I watch as Alyssa fusses with her hair and then carefully puts on some eyeliner. "Now remember," I tell her, "I'll text you when you're next in line, so you'll only have a couple of minutes to get to the choir room."

Alyssa nods nervously. "I don't know if I can sing. I'm going to be so nervous."

"It doesn't matter. The important thing is that you leave right away after you're done. Got it?"

"Yes, for the tenth time, I've got it." Alyssa glances out the window. "Hitch, some of your hens are in the garage."

I groan. "That idiot. He must have left the coop open. That's okay. He'll have to clean up the mess."

Alyssa presses her nose against the glass. "I think they're attacking a rabbit or something. It's all bloody. Yuck. I didn't know hens were carnivores."

I peek out the window. The hens are viciously pecking at something. A sickening feeling comes over me. I can see my unzipped backpack hanging half in, half out of the open car door. Two hens are fighting to stick their heads inside it. Derek must have gone into the car for some reason and left the door open.

Wait a minute. I didn't leave my backpack open. Then, I remember the silent conversation at the kitchen table. This is no accident. It's payback. A hen suddenly swivels her head, and I swear she stares at me in the window. And winks.

Then I'm running, taking the stairs two at a time, with Alyssa right behind me. As we burst outside, I can see the hens aren't killing a rabbit at all. They're killing the Cute Red Wig. Some of the hens carried the plastic bag outside and shredded it with their beaks. Now they're fighting over the wig, dragging it through the mud. And I can see, clear as day, they're inching toward a huge mound of fresh chicken poop.

How could I be so stupid? Those devil birds were never simple barnyard animals. The ladies hate me and they're out to get me. I never should have doubted it. They've hatched another plot behind my back—one last dirty scheme to try to ruin my life.

I give a last burst of speed, splashing through mud puddles, screaming at the hens. Just as I reach them, they scoot away with triumphant cackles. I slowly pick up a wet, muddy, crap-smeared tangle that used to be a wig. I hear a groan, but I'm not sure if it's me or Alyssa. I glance back toward the house. Luckily, my parents haven't noticed anything. Alyssa holds her nose. I grab the water hose and spray off the worst of the poop and grime.

"What are we going to do?" Alyssa moans.

My brain is in high panic mode. I take a deep breath and try to think. "We still have time. We can fix this."

"Fix it? Look at that thing! It's ruined!"

The Cute Red Wig can no longer be called cute. Or red. It looks more like a drowned rat. "Come on, let's get it inside."

I know Derek is probably watching from a window, laughing to himself. Luckily, he's clueless about the missing wig or he would have already tattled to my parents. Anyway, I can't worry about him right now. I tuck the wig inside my backpack and we race upstairs to the bathroom and lock the door. Alyssa grabs the blow-dryer and blasts the wig while I towel off the worst parts. The curls turn to instant frizz.

"Curling iron!" Alyssa barks. Alyssa may not be a whiz at math—or science or English—but she's a hairstyling genius. She can cut, curl, crimp, updo, and braid like a pro. I slap the curling iron into her hand.

"Kate!" my mother calls from downstairs. "Time to go!"

"In a minute!" I shout.

Alyssa hefts a lock of the wig in her hand. "Some kind of synthetic fiber," she mutters. "I hope it's heat resistant." She tests the iron, then rolls up a lock of hair. Right away it sizzles and the smell of burned plastic fills the bathroom. Alyssa quickly untwists the hair, but half the curl sticks to the curling iron.

"You scalped it!" I yelp.

"It's not my fault! It's a cheap synthetic! Look, at least I tested it in back." Alyssa twists the wig for me to see. "It won't even show in front."

She lowers the heat, then gingerly tries another curl. This time the wig doesn't burn, but the curl looks like a perm that's gone bad. Way bad.

"Kate!" my mother calls from downstairs.

"In a minute!" I shout back. I know we've only got one more call, and then my mother will be coming up the stairs for me.

"Hurry," I prod.

"Do you want to do it?" Alyssa snaps. I don't, so I watch over her shoulder as she works. "It doesn't curl like regular hair," she complains. "I don't think this wig is meant to be styled. You're not supposed to get it wet," she adds accusingly.

"What was I supposed to do, leave the chicken poop? That would be kind of a giveaway, wouldn't it? Everyone would know I took it."

"You did take it," Alyssa retorts.

I glance at her to see if she's having second thoughts.

She grins at me and dangles the wig. "Crapkate Walden strikes again." The strange-looking curls bounce up and down. It looks more like a synthetic snarl than a curly red wig.

"The plastic head sits way in the back of the room by

the window," I say, trying to sound positive. "No one will even notice."

"Kate!" my mother yells up the stairs. "RIGHT NOW!"

"We're coming!"

I pop the wig into another plastic bag. The image of the hens fighting to get into my backpack comes back to me as I stow the wig. What were they after? I search inside my pack and find bread crumbs scattered everywhere. Derek. Grudgingly, I have to admit his plan shows a certain evil genius.

That doesn't stop me from telling my mother what happened when we're in the car. "They dragged my stuff out into the yard and ruined it!"

"I guess Derek needs more practice feeding the hens," my mother says. "Two weeks ought to do it."

Derek starts to whine, then snaps shut his mouth after a warning look from our mother. He and I glare at each other.

"Did you hear the thunder last night?" my mother asks in her *let's-be-pleasant* voice. "We're supposed to have more bad storms this afternoon."

The sun glares off the windshield, without a cloud in sight. It's sticky and hot for October. Everyone says we're having an extralong summer this year. The tree leaves are usually flaming orange and yellow by this time, but they've only barely begun to turn. Small bursts of color stain the trees like someone went crazy shooting off a paintball gun.

Suddenly, I feel nostalgic. We started shooting *Night of*

the Zombie Chickens almost exactly a year ago. In one of the first scenes we shot, a zombie hurries down the road, searching for Mallory. As soon as it's out of sight, Alyssa pops out of a big, colorful mound of leaves and runs the other way. It's one of the movie's more scenic moments. Then I think of Margaret's hair glowing like fire as she walks down the road toward the sunset. That was pretty spectacular, too.

I can't help wondering if Margaret would be so eager to help return the wig if she knew Alyssa wants me to reshoot the end of my movie. If I use the ending with Margaret, Alyssa will be upset. If I cut the ending and reshoot, Margaret will be hurt. My heart starts thumping and a dull pain throbs at the base of my skull as we pull up to school. I decide I can only worry about one thing at a time. My movie will have to wait. First, we have to save my neck and restore Alyssa's honor. Let the auditions begin.

34

Alyssa and I split up. She goes to her locker and I head straight to the music room. Despite all our planning last week, I never actually signed up to audition. Luckily, the sign-up sheet is still hanging on the wall. It looks like the name of almost every female seventh grader is on it. I scrawl my own at the bottom of the list.

"Hello, Kate."

I jump about a foot at Mr. Cantrell's voice right behind me. He has one of those quiet gazes that make you feel nervous, like he knows something and he's just waiting for you to come out and admit it.

"Hi, Mr. Cantrell. I was just signing up for auditions."

"Good, good," he says vaguely. "I was just coming to get the list."

I untape it from the wall and hand it to him.

"Oh, my." He riffles through the pages and smiles weakly. "Lots of interest, I see."

"It's too bad about the wig," I say, and then immediately want to kick myself. It's a well-known fact that criminals often return to the scene of their crime. They also have an obsessive need to talk about what they did. Here I am, hardly twenty feet from the bald plastic head, blabbing away. But Mr. Cantrell merely nods.

"Yes, it is too bad."

"You know, I don't think Alyssa took it," I say in a rush. "She's not the type to steal stuff. And why would she want the wig, anyway?"

"I certainly hope you're right, Kate."

"It was probably just someone playing a practical joke," I blindly go on. "Now that rehearsals will be starting soon, I bet whoever took it will put it back."

Mr. Cantrell gives me another wistful smile and departs with the list. I treat myself to a good hard pinch for giving away the plot like an amateur. But seeing his sad face makes me feel even guiltier. Poor Mr. Cantrell probably took the theft personally, like a slap in the face. He's probably devastated that someone would stoop so low as to take the red wig for his musical. I can only hope he'll feel better once the wig is returned.

At lunchtime I sit with Margaret and Doris, as usual. Alyssa and I decided we would pretend to still be mad at each other until we got the wig safely back on its plastic head.

"I wish I could help," Doris says for the hundredth time, "but I don't sing. And I have Math Club after school."

I didn't even know our school had a math club. I'm tempted to ask what they do, exactly, but Doris has her mouth full and I decide not to chance it.

"That's okay. You're the mastermind," I tell her. "The mastermind never gets her hands dirty with the gritty details."

"Did you tell Alyssa about the ending to your movie?" Margaret asks me.

She says it casually but I feel an icy finger in my stomach. Margaret has figured out that if Alyssa and I become friends again, then Alyssa might want to finish *Night of the Zombie Chickens*.

I always wished my life could be a movie, but now I'm not so sure. Even I can't keep up with all these plot threads. "Um, yeah. She thought it sounded . . . interesting. Once she sees it, she'll love it," I babble on.

Margaret smiles, cheered.

I try to smile back, but it's hard. Frogs are jumping in my stomach, and the thought of singing in front of Mr. Cantrell makes me want to puke. I push away my sandwich. There's no way I can eat anything today.

The afternoon crawls by. In history class I gaze out the window, hiding a yawn. Huge clouds hang in the air like floating sledgehammers. When I glance back at the clock, I'm almost positive it's gone backward.

By business ed class at the end of the day, all the sledge-hammers have blended together and the last bit of blue sky has disappeared. The wind churns in the trees and leaves scatter everywhere. A hard rain begins to drive against the windows.

As we leave class, Alyssa bumps into me and whispers in my ear: "There's a severe thunderstorm warning. I hope Mr. Cantrell doesn't cancel auditions!"

I shrug like I'm not worried. A small part of me wishes he *would* cancel so I don't have to humiliate myself. When I drag myself to the choir room, it seems like the entire seventh-grade female population is waiting in the hallway, and a lot of eighth graders, too. They all watch me as I check the audition schedule. Sure enough, with a last name of Walden, I'm second to last in line, right before Margaret Yorkel.

"I heard there's a tornado watch," Margaret says at my elbow. She smiles and I can feel the eyes of every single girl on me.

"Cool," I say loudly. "Maybe we'll all get blown away."

It looks like it's going to be a long wait. Luckily, the music department is tucked away at the end of a wing because most of the girls are sprawled on the hallway floor, chatting, texting, or doing homework. I dump my backpack, slip off my shoes, and join them. It takes all my concentration just to try to look relaxed. Mr. Cantrell is doing the auditions in the choir room. The music classroom, where the bald plastic head sits, is just two doors away.

A huge crack of thunder makes everyone jump. Lydia and Tina Turlick both scream and collapse on the floor. Mr. Cantrell emerges from the choir room and frowns.

"Please, girls, keep it down. Jennifer Adams?"

Jennifer bounces into the choir room behind Mr. Cantrell. Mr. Cantrell has decided that everyone should sing the same song to make it easier. We hear the piano plunk out "Tomorrow." Jennifer's voice screeches on the top note.

Lydia makes a face like a constipated opera singer and everyone laughs. It occurs to me that being second to last isn't such a bad thing.

I was worried about getting through the song since I hadn't exactly prepared, but after hearing fifteen auditions in a row, I know the words well enough to sing in my sleep. When Debbie Jacobs goes in, I slip away to the bathroom and text Alyssa. *You're next.*

By the time Alyssa arrives, Debbie is just leaving the choir room. Mr. Cantrell pokes his head out. "Alyssa Jensen?"

Every pair of eyes is glued on Alyssa as she walks through the crowded hallway to the door. Luckily, Mr. Cantrell waits for her because the crowd's mood is ugly. I think I would have sagged under the weight of all those eyes and sunk right through the floor. Alyssa keeps her head up and her eyes straight in front of her, but her cheeks flood with red.

As soon as the door closes, Tina Turlick makes a nasty face, which isn't very different from her normal face. "I can't believe Mr. Cantrell is letting her try out! She should be banned from the play."

"We should chop off all her hair, dye it red, and make a new wig," Sarah Perkins adds.

Lydia gives a huge gasp, like she's just come up with the perfect idea. "Yeah, let's scalp her! I always wanted to scalp somebody."

Everyone falls quiet then as Alyssa's voice rises on the chorus of "Tomorrow." She's a little pitchy, but you can hardly blame her. She knows everyone is listening and talking a mile a minute about her. I close my eyes and say a little prayer that our plan will work. I need to clear Alyssa's name fast or she'll crack under all the pressure. My heart sinks as I remember the condition of the Not-So-Cute Red Wig. Even if we manage to safely return it, I have to face facts—no one is going to want to put that thing on her head. The uproar would continue, only now it would be about who destroyed the wig. The best I can do is make sure nobody suspects Alyssa any longer.

Alyssa sails out the door and I hold my breath. Will she remember her lines?

"Thanks, Mr. Cantrell!" she says loudly. "I've got to run! I have a doctor's appointment. I'm already late!"

So far, so good. Everyone knows she's leaving the building.

"Maddie Long?" Mr. Cantrell calls out. He's holding the door open, and through it we can see sheets of rain spraying the windows.

"'I have a doctor's appointment,'" Tina mimics. "She doesn't want to hang out here with the rest of us."

The rain has given me an idea. I casually pick up my backpack. My eyes meet Margaret's for a split second and then I take a few steps down to the music classroom. Luckily, the door has a pane of glass and through it, I can see the big wall of windows on the far side of the room. The rain and the whipping wind outside look pretty impressive.

"Wow!" I say loudly. "It looks really nasty out there."

A few girls glance over my way, but I'm too low on the social totem pole for them to pay much attention. I need Lydia. I take a deep breath and take my game, and my decibel level, up a notch.

"Hey, Lydia," I call out, so loud that everyone looks over. "You might have to audition during a tornado." I nod toward the music classroom window.

"Cool," Lydia calls out. "Maybe it'll suck me up and I won't have to sing!"

Just what I'm afraid of—I got her attention for a millisecond, but not enough to make her get up and come over. I lick my lips. I need to deliver an Oscar-winning performance and I'm running out of time. Lydia is up next to audition. Luckily, everyone is tired of hearing endless renditions of "Tomorrow."

I flinch like something big just flew past the window. "Holy crap, what was that?" I exclaim. "I think a house just flew by! Too bad we're not trying out for *The Wizard of Oz!*"

I say a private *Hallelujah* as Lydia laughs, then bounces up and strolls over. Immediately, five other girls follow, then four more. Pretty soon, everyone is trying to peer through the small window in the door. Hens act pretty much the same way. They're impossible to herd, but if you can get the leader to follow you, the rest will tag along.

I grab the knob to throw open the door so everyone can go inside and that's when I realize I'm in big trouble. The door is locked. Mr. Cantrell must have started locking it since the theft of the wig. My head starts swirling like the leaves outside the window. If the door is locked, then I can't get in to replace the wig. I glance at Margaret. She bites her lip, looking worried.

"That's some seriously nasty weather," Lydia agrees, peering through the door.

Just then, Mr. Cantrell pops his head into the hallway and consults his list. "Lydia Merritt?"

My brain is frozen. I can't think of what to do. Then, Margaret's voice sings out.

"Mr. Cantrell, have you seen how bad the weather is? We want to look through the windows, but we can't get in."

I rattle the door for effect. Some of the others chime in and suddenly it's a game. The girls on the outside of the pack start jumping up and down like they're trying to see in. "Come on, Mr. C!" they call. "We want to see the big storm."

Mr. Cantrell glances at his list of names. Luckily, there's one thing I know about teachers. Deep down, they all want to be cool. They want to be liked by their students. I think that's why Mr. Cantrell finally shrugs and smiles. "It *is* ugly out there."

My knees practically sag with relief as he unlocks the door. Thank goodness for Margaret. Everyone spills inside and *ooh*s and *aah*s at the black sheets of rain pouring down. The windows shake like they're possessed by evil demon chickens.

I cross over to the window with the others and then accidentally on purpose knock over the bald head. "Oops," I say cheerfully. "Poor bald, plastic head."

Margaret laughs loudly. "We should buy her a hat!"

No one laughs much, but we've made our point. The wig is still missing.

"Okay, girls," Mr. Cantrell calls. "We still have lots of auditions. Let's go. Lydia, you're up next."

Lydia smirks and suddenly everyone is rushing out behind her, eager to hear her sing. Margaret makes sure everyone gets out and then nods to me as she leaves. She will watch the door for me. Moving quickly, I grab the wig out of my backpack, fluff up the limp curls as best I can, stick it onto the plastic head, and then shove the head against the windows. Maybe if the wig is in silhouette, people won't notice the sorry shape it's in.

Luckily, everyone is listening breathlessly to Lydia sing. I ease open the door and slip out without anyone noticing.

In my short time on earth, I've already observed that life can be flat-out wrong sometimes—the prettiest girls also end up having the best voices, or they rock in gymnastics, or they're ballerinas and star in *The Nutcracker Suite,* or all of the above. I'm not sure who makes up the rules, but I'm pretty sure that "Life is fair" isn't one of them. I'd already made up my mind that Lydia would get the part of Annie. That's just how life works.

Usually. As I glance around, nobody dares to snicker but I see definite grins. A steam cloud of relief rises up from our huddled masses as Lydia yowls her way through the chorus. She might be funny, but she's no Little Orphan Annie.

Still, when she swaggers out of the choir room and pops her gum, everybody laughs like she's just cracked the funniest joke ever. "*Sayonara*, ladies," Lydia calls with a wave. "I'm off to surf the tsunami."

Thunder cracks overhead as if on cue. "Don't drown," Tina calls, and everybody nervously laughs.

Mr. Cantrell calls out another name and the next victim follows him into the choir room. Roughly half the girls are now gone. I decide to wait for a few more auditions before "discovering" the wig. Only a few girls need to see it. The rest of the class will hear about it in a nanosecond or two once the first text message goes out.

As we head into the names that start with *S*, Margaret suddenly starts telling me how she's redecorating her room. "Do you want to come see it when it's done?" She talks fast and her eyes dart around the hall. We're both nervous. I can tell she's trying to figure out how to "discover" the wig without raising suspicions. Suddenly, the storm lets loose with a humongous boom of thunder.

Margaret jumps up and screams. "Did you hear that?"

She runs back to the music room door and peers through the window. I follow behind her and so do a few of the other girls. We gaze out the window, exclaiming how dark it is— and seriously, it is dark and scary-looking by now. I want to blurt out something about the wig, but I know I have to be careful. After all, I'm the one who pointed out the bald head earlier. If I mention the wig now, it will be too on the nose. That's a script-writing term for "too obvious."

Margaret must be hoping the others will notice the wig because she doesn't say anything, either. The problem is, it's so dark outside that the whole room is deep in shadow. Even *I* can hardly see the wig, and I know it's there.

It helps to have God in your special effects department because I'm pretty sure he lets loose with a whopper of a lightning bolt just then. It floods the entire room until it glows whitish blue. Margaret catches her breath. Did she notice the wig's sorry condition? *I haven't had a chance to tell her about that yet.* Thunder rattles the windows. *I'm starting to feel like I'm in a horror flick—Curse of the Werewig.*

"Did you see that?" Cindy Syvert suddenly asks.

"Yeah, that was huge," I say innocently.

Cindy presses her face against the glass. "No, look, it's the wig! I think the wig is back!"

"No way!" Holly Taylor screeches.

We all peer through the window. A moment of doubt, then I say, "You're right, I see it!" *Maybe I should skip directing and go into acting. I definitely seem to have a knack for it.*

"That's too weird," Margaret pipes up. "It wasn't there just twenty minutes ago, remember?"

Holly opens the door as another burst of lightning floods the room.

"Wait!" I cry.

The last thing I want is for them to inspect the wig. I was tempted to leave the door locked just so this wouldn't happen, but I finally decided to leave it wedged open. That way, it looks like someone could have snuck in and returned the wig while the rest of us weren't paying attention.

"We should tell Mr. Cantrell right away!" Margaret chimes in quickly. "Before anyone messes with it."

Holly is still staring at it. "You know, I'm not sure that's the wig. Does it look funny to you?"

"Definitely the Cute Red Wig," I reassure her. "It's just dark in there. Come on, let's tell Mr. Cantrell." I close the door until I hear the click of the tumblers falling into place. For now, the wig is safe from prying eyes.

Mr. Cantrell pokes his head out of the choir room to motion another girl inside. He looks tired and his hair is rumpled like he's been pulling his hands through it.

"Mr. Cantrell!" Holly practically screams. "The wig is back! Someone put it back!"

"No way!" Tina Turlick howls. She and the five remaining girls stampede to the door.

Everyone stares at the wig from the doorway. All I can say is, it's a good thing it's on the other side of the room, in deep shadow.

"Alyssa snuck it back in!" Tina says.

I hold my breath. This is the fateful moment. There's nothing worse for a director than to carefully plant clues in a movie, only to have the audience miss them. Were they paying attention?

Then Holly shakes her head. "Alyssa couldn't have done it. She was already gone."

"That's right," Linda Uecker agrees. "Remember, we came to look out the windows and the wig wasn't there. Wasn't that after Alyssa left?"

Now it's my turn. I chime in like I'm just following along. "Yeah, she was gone. She had a doctor's appointment or something."

I'm telling you, Angelina Jolie couldn't have delivered that line better. It had just the right amount of bored dead-pan to give it the ring of truth. Not that I'm bragging.

"Oh my gosh," Margaret says. "That means Alyssa really didn't take the wig. And all this time everyone's been accusing her and she was telling the truth—"

Wow. Her innocent surprise almost tops my performance.

"That's weird," Tina says with a shrug. "I wonder who did it, then."

And just like that, victory is achieved.

I turn my back on the wig. "Uh, Mr. Cantrell, not to rush you, but the weather's getting really bad and I have to be somewhere soon. Do you know how much longer?"

All this time, Mr. Cantrell has been staring at the wig with a strange look on his face. I can't tell if he's surprised, suspicious, relieved, or just dazed from hearing "Tomorrow" thirty-six times in a row. He comes to and checks his watch. "Yes, it's getting late. Let's finish up, girls."

"Isn't that amazing, Mr. Cantrell?" Margaret gushes. "I bet someone was just playing a prank, and now they brought it back. And here everyone thought Alyssa did it but she didn't."

"That is something, isn't it?" Mr. Cantrell says.

We troop back toward the choir room. The other girls have already whipped out their phones, and I know the entire seventh grade will know within minutes. A jury of Alyssa Jensen's peers has thrown out her guilty verdict. Court is now adjourned.

35

I slide down the wall and sink to the floor, suddenly exhausted. In the choir room, Mr. Cantrell plunks out the first chords of "Tomorrow" yet again. I really wish it *were* tomorrow.

There will still be plenty of talk about what happened to the Cute Red Wig, but at least no one will be blaming Alyssa. Or me. You'd think I'd be feeling pretty great by this time. My plan went off without a hitch. Alyssa's name has been cleared. But something's eating at me down in my belly. I figure it's hunger, so I buy a candy bar from the vending machine and munch on it. Still, the feeling doesn't go away. Something's wrong, but I have to chew on it for a while before I figure out what's bothering me.

My mother advised me to tell my "friend" to return the stolen item and admit the truth. I did tell Alyssa, but Mr. Cantrell is the one I actually stole from. I swallow hard. I want to be the kind of person who does the right thing. On the other hand, I definitely *don't* want to be the kind of person who gets in trouble for stealing.

All my fancy footwork this afternoon doesn't change the fact that the wig is now ruined. I could blame the chickens or Derek, but even I'm not quite that lame. The ache in my stomach turns into a gut-pounder as I realize Mr. Cantrell deserves to know what happened to his wig.

I wish there were more girls in front of me to delay the painful moment, but there are only three of us left. I didn't think the storm could get much worse, but it has. I can barely hear Linda Uecker's quavery soprano over the howling wind. She hurries out, ashen-faced, and then it's my turn. I've just heard the song a bazillion times, but suddenly I can't remember the first line. In fact, I can't remember a single word except *tomorrow*. Another funny thing. I can't get up. It feels like someone has superglued me to the floor.

Margaret leans over. "Don't worry, you'll do great. Don't be nervous."

"Kate?" Mr. Cantrell stands in the doorway. I drag myself up and follow him inside. We both stare out the windows. I've never seen such black clouds throwing down so much rain. I decide I'll audition first and then confess my crime afterward.

Mr. Cantrell sits at the piano and plays the familiar chords, but the gale-force wind and the rattling windows are way louder than my voice. At least Margaret won't hear me. Of course, neither will Mr. Cantrell. I need to sing louder. I push the words out of my throat as hard as I can, hoping I'm hitting a few notes along the way. Mr. Cantrell's eye twitches, but he gamely plays on.

Just before the chorus, I hear a strange, muted groan coming from outside. At first I think it's the wind. As the sound climbs to a wail, I realize it's the tornado siren. We're almost finished, though, so Mr. Cantrell doesn't stop and neither do I. The siren, the wind, and I all shriek together, until finally it's over.

"Uh, thank you, Kate." Mr. Cantrell wipes his forehead.

The loudspeaker erupts just then, announcing a tornado warning has been issued and everyone in the building needs to move into a central hallway. Before I can explain anything, Mr. Cantrell herds Margaret and me into the corridor. We plunk down along with a few stray kids. The nervous chatter trails off as thunder booms overhead. It feels like the hallway is shaking. We hear a loud smash of breaking glass from somewhere down the hall. That's when my heart starts pounding. A girl screams and a boy tries to climb inside a locker and gets stuck. Mr. Cantrell tries to calm everyone, but his face is pasty white, covered by a sheen of sweat. Not exactly reassuring.

I take a deep breath. Maybe if I tell Mr. Cantrell right

now, he'll be so distracted by the storm that he'll forget to expel me.

"Mr. Cantrell?" Margaret suddenly raises her hand like she's in class. "Can I audition for you while we're waiting?"

I can only stare at her. Is she from another planet? Does she really expect him to wheel the piano into the hall-way? Mr. Cantrell nods, dazed. Margaret stands up and smoothes down her skirt. She starts to sing, without accompaniment, in the middle of a tornado, with kids gaping and Mr. Cantrell sweating. And it turns out freckle-faced Margaret Yorkel can sing.

I think my mouth actually drops open. Something like relief washes over Mr. Cantrell's face as he listens to Margaret. I'm pretty certain he's just found his Annie.

Plenty of students were probably praying a tornado would sweep the school away, but in the end the storm just dies out. The wind quiets and the voice on the loudspeaker gives the all clear. Mr. Cantrell, Margaret, and I wander down the hall to see where the breaking glass sound came from.

The music classroom looks like it's been visited by its very own personal tornado. Two of the big plate glass windows are smashed and there's glass everywhere. A blizzard of papers and trash blanket the room. As we crowd in to survey the damage, I notice it first—a dented plastic head lying on the floor. I glance out the jagged windowpane just in time to see a scrap of red bounce through the parking lot. The three of us silently watch as it snakes along the ground, jumps into the air, cartwheels across the soccer field, and flies away over the trees.

Finally, it shrinks to a tiny speck and disappears. After all my plotting and planning, the Cute Red Wig is history. I'm not sure whether I feel like laughing or crying. Mr. Cantrell's face looks equally amazed. Even Margaret seems struck speechless.

"Can you believe that?" she finally murmurs.

Mr. Cantrell smiles wanly at us. "I guess that wig just wasn't meant to be in our musical, girls."

Margaret and Mr. Cantrell peer out the window, as if hoping the red mop will reappear, but I know it's gone for good. I grin as a gust of wind tousles Margaret's hair. As it turns out, I'm pretty sure we don't need that red wig anyway.

And then it hits me—I'm off the hook. I tried to do the right thing, but the wig is gone, despite my best efforts. Is God giving me a pardon? *Don't waste it,* a voice says inside my head.

So did I get away with something? Maybe. I endured plenty of punishment, though. And I've learned some things. In my wildest dreams, I never would have scripted a storm as the ultimate thief, which makes me think, who needs movies? Life has more than enough bizarre plot twists. And just like quirky characters make a movie more fun, quirky friends do the same. Which is why I think everyone needs at least one friend who loves Math Club and laughs like a congested goose.

Mr. Cantrell turns away from the window. "Well, that's that," he says.

Even I can't think of a better closing line.

36

The next day, everyone treats Alyssa especially nice to make up for accusing her of being a low-life thief. When I sit down with Margaret and Doris at lunch, I see Alyssa hesitate. There's a seat open next to Lydia and she waves Alyssa over.

I'm really glad that Alyssa and I have gone back to being friends, but things aren't exactly the same as before. I guess they can't be, because we're not exactly the same people. Before, I just wanted to have my little group of friends at school and not rock the boat. Then I got kicked out of the boat and all the rules changed. The old me might have worried about whether Alyssa was okay with sitting next to Margaret and Doris at lunch. Now I just wait to see what she will do.

Alyssa waves back to Lydia and then heads over to sit next to me. Mimi and Lizzy gape, but they follow her. At first it's awkward, but everyone gets along, just as I thought they would.

I come to think of Alyssa's friendship with Lydia as a kind of sickness—a rare, exotic flu that she's recovered from. I watch for signs of a relapse, but she seems to have built up a strong immunity to Lydia. Sometimes when we make plans, it's just the two of us. But other times, Mimi and Lizzy join us with Margaret and Doris, and then it's pure craziness, especially when Doris decides something is funny.

And Lydia, of course, remains Lydia. I can't really dislike her. In small doses she's fun. You just can't count on her for anything, including friendship. She gets her ears double-pierced, puts red streaks in her hair, and still calls me Mrs. Director.

There's only one thing still bothering me. The baby monitor sits upstairs in my bedroom, hidden inside my closet. I haven't had the courage to use it. Now, with the wig out of the way, it's time. I know spying on my dad is bad. I must be a bad kid, then, because I can't help it. I have to know.

I sneak into his office one afternoon after school and plant the plastic base, which transmits the sounds. After looking around, I finally hide it in a bushy fake ivy near his desk.

That evening, my mother asks my father about his day.

He's gazing out the window and doesn't even hear her, until she repeats the question.

"Dull," he answers. "Just like yesterday. Too many meetings. Too many numbers. I think I need a vacation. Or maybe a brand-new Mustang convertible." He winks at Derek.

"Yeah!" Derek shouts.

I narrow my eyes. My dad craves change and excitement. He wants to buy a new, expensive toy. He sounds like a midlife crisis poster child. Does he want a new family to go with the new car?

"By the way," my dad says casually, "I have a business trip coming up."

My mother brightens. "Remember, we talked about my going with you on one of your trips? Maybe this would be a good time to—"

"Not this time," my dad cuts her off. "It's to Indiana. It's going to be very boring."

After dinner, he disappears into the den. My mother watches him go, a small frown crinkling between her eyes. So she's noticed, too.

I run up to my room, lock the door, and turn on the monitor. It crackles a moment, then my dad's voice springs into the air like he's standing in the room with me. "Third quarter's down. Yeah. Six-point-two percent. Give me the differential. Okay, how about Howie's sector? Five-point-nine? Ouch. Okay."

As I listen to him spiel off random numbers, it sounds like poetry. I breathe the hugest sigh of relief in the world. He really is doing office work. And it sounds pretty darn boring.

"Okay, thanks, John. Bye."

I hear the tiny beep-beep-beep of his cell phone and then his chair creaking. I lean forward to turn off the monitor.

"Well, hello, Junie. How are you this fine evening?"

I freeze. I hardly recognize my dad's voice, it's so changed. It sounds teasing, flirty... undadlike.

"Please give me some good news. Tell me you got our tickets to Bali. I've been thinking about it all day." He gives a low chuckle.

So that's it. I sink to the floor. I can't breathe, can't think. That low-down, cheating rat. When I think of my unsuspecting mother, tears well up in my eyes. She will be crushed. He's going to tear apart our family, all for some bimbo named Junie.

"I know. That gave me a scare," he goes on. "I thought she found out. But we're okay." He pauses. "Sure, the kids will be upset about being left behind, but I'll explain it to them."

He sounds so... nonchalant. How can a person be so two-faced? I'm so steaming mad that I'm ready to march downstairs and thump him over the head with the monitor. Then, sadness overwhelms me and all I can do is listen, tears streaming down my face.

My dad croons, "I can't believe this is finally going to happen. After all our planning." He chuckles. "I'll tell Jean you're the one who did it all."

I grimace. Did what all? Stole his heart and destroyed our family? Does my mother know this woman?

"She is going to be thrilled. You only turn forty once, right? Oh, it'll be a surprise, believe me. And the hotel is booked, too? Fantastic. I know this has been a lot more work than you expected, after that first trip fell through. You're an angel, Junie, doing this on your own time. You do such a great job on our business travel, I knew you were the one to call."

I frown at the monitor, not sure I heard right. These things should come with a rewind button. What did he say? Then, it slowly sinks in. My mother's birthday is in January, just a few months away. My father's taking a trip, but not with Junie. He must be planning a surprise vacation for my mother's fortieth birthday.

Relief washes over me like a strong river as I realize my dad is exactly the man I thought he was. I just sit for a moment, eyes closed, as my fears slip free and float away. I suddenly feel wonderfully light. Then the first pang of guilt hits. How could I think my father would ever do such a terrible thing?

I throw down the monitor, fling open my door, run downstairs, and burst into his office. He stands up, alarmed at the tears still on my face. "Kate, what's wrong?"

I fly into his arms and cling to him. He wraps his arms around me, and I wish I could stay there forever.

He strokes my hair, his voice worried. "Baby, what's the matter? What's wrong? Tell me what it is."

I start bawling again because he's so worried about me and it's so sweet and I'm so relieved. Pretty soon, though, I'm laughing and assuring him that nothing's wrong. "I'm just happy," I tell him.

My dad sinks into his chair. "Happy? Are you sure, Katie? You gave me quite a scare."

"I'm really happy—that's all."

I kiss the top of his head, and if he thinks *Teenage hormones*, at least he doesn't say it out loud.

37

Just as I thought, Alyssa is upset when I decide not to reshoot the end of *Night of the Zombie Chickens*. Luckily, the more she gets to know Margaret, the less she seems to care. The truth is, it just doesn't feel right cutting Margaret out. It would be like admitting that she was just a last-ditch idea to patch together my movie. Maybe it did start out that way, but the more I look at the footage, the more I like it. It's the absolute perfect ending for *Night of the Zombie Chickens*.

It takes me a month, but I finally finish the entire movie, with music and sound effects and everything. My parents even offer to rent the old Roxy Theater downtown for an evening so I can put on a real premiere. At first, I didn't think there were enough people to invite to bother. By the time I make a list of everyone who acted in it, though, the list is pretty long. Then the newspaper somehow gets hold of the story. I suspect my mother called it.

A reporter actually calls up and interviews me. Their photographer snaps a photo of me holding a chicken, and I show up on page three under the headline YOUNG DIRECTOR SETS SIGHTS ON HOLLYWOOD. All of a sudden, everyone at school is asking about my movie and they think it's cool we have chickens. Go figure.

At the theater on the night of the premiere, my mother gives me a huge grin, then whips out a cardboard sign. It reads: TICKETS: ADULTS $3, STUDENTS $2. And underneath that: TICKET SALES WILL HELP FUND KATE'S NEXT MOVIE.

"I wasn't going to charge people to get in," I tell her.

"Nonsense. It's for a great cause. People will be happy to pay." My mother arranges the sign on a table and places a money box next to it.

"That's a great deal," my dad chimes in. "Your movie is worth way more than that."

He pulls out a twenty and winks at me as he throws it in the money box.

I throw my arms around my mother and give her a hug. I'm surprised how happy she looks as she hugs me back. My dad smiles at my mom, and I can't believe that I ever thought he was cheating on her. They may have their problems, but that's not one of them. I hug my dad and he whispers in my ear, "We're really proud of you."

I'm supernervous. I just know that no one's going to come. The reporter will take a photo of an empty theater and publish it in the newspaper for the whole town to see.

People slowly start to trickle in. Pretty soon, I can't believe how many have shown up. The picnic zombies all wave at me. Even Mr. Cantrell is there, along with some of my other teachers. A lot of kids from school make it, including Lydia and her gang. And everybody takes out their wallet like it's no big deal. After they read the sign, some even throw in a few extra bucks.

Finally, the big moment arrives. The theater goes dark. The voices quiet. I hear a loud giggle, which has to be Lydia.

Night of the Zombie Chickens is no Hollywood block-buster, but it gets some laughs, mostly at the right times, and it has some semi-scary moments, too. When Mallory whips off her ski mask at the end and it's Margaret, a mur-mur of surprise runs through the crowd. I'm happy that my twist ending worked.

My parents told me that, as the director, I should go up afterward and thank everyone who helped with the movie. So at the end, I slowly mount the stairs to the stage, feel-ing like my knees will give out. I clear my throat and thank everyone for coming out. When I thank my parents for their help, I can feel myself starting to choke up. A few tears prickle my eyelids as I realize it's really over. My first movie is finished. One day, when I'm a big Hollywood director, I hope people will say that *Night of the Zombie Chickens* was made during my formative years. I like the sound of that.

I ask Alyssa to come up, and when I introduce her as Mallory, everyone gives a huge round of applause. Then I call out Margaret's name. She joins us, blushing as red as her hair, and I introduce her as the other Mallory. Even the kids at school clap wildly for her. Alyssa grins at Margaret, then grabs her hand and they raise their arms up over their heads. I've never seen Margaret smile so big. There aren't any fancy actors or red carpets, but I feel like my first movie premiere ever has been a big success.

Afterward, I'm amazed as I count all the money. For my next movie, I will finally have a real budget!

Everyone except me is shocked when Margaret Yorkel gets the lead for *Annie*. Tina Turlick even mutters that it's just because her hair is red and Mr. Cantrell can't afford another wig. Then Tina hears Margaret sing and that shuts her up. Two weeks after my movie premiere, Alyssa, Doris, and I go to the opening night of the school musical. Margaret rocks the house, just like I knew she would. I like to tell everyone that I discovered her first.

Afterward, the four of us go to Twisters for a burger.

"Isn't it funny how we went through all that for nothing?" Margaret says as we wait for our food. "All that work, and the Cute Red Wig just flies off in a storm."

And that's when an idea hits me with the force of a

volcanic cataclysm. I have to catch my breath as I picture it—zombies in wigs. It's the perfect sequel. I'll call it *Red Wig in a Storm*. Now all I need is a tornado, a big glass window, and blood. Lots of blood.

ACKNOWLEDGMENTS

I wish to say a special thank you to:

My daughters, Daniela and Rebecca, for letting me listen in on their lives—the tears, the tumult, and, most of all, the laughs.

My critique partner, Diane Swanson, for all her invaluable insights, which made this a better story, and for her most egg-cellent friendship.

My beta readers, for bravely wading through early drafts and for all their thoughtful feedback: Annika Swanson, Carly and Lauri Miranda, and Sofia and Colleen White.

Ben and Lyssa King, who provided friendship, support, wise counsel, and delicious food, all at crucial moments along the way.

My agent, Catherine Drayton, and editor, Emily Meehan, for all their talents in bringing this project to life, and for getting the humor and believing in it.

And, of course, to Henrietta, Agatha, and all the Ladies, without whom this book never would have hatched.

KEEP READING FOR A SNEAK PEEK AT:

All the cafeteria lunches at Medford Junior High taste like they've been boiled in a rusty cauldron, but the hot dogs are the worst. The cafeteria lady keeps them swimming in a greasy vat of lukewarm water and by the time you bite into one, it's cold and rubbery. Normally, I squirt on globs of mustard and choke it down, but for some reason today I just can't bite into something that looks like a leftover body part. I throw my hot dog down on my tray and it rolls off the stale bun, falls from the table, and bounces on the floor. Alyssa snickers, Lizzy makes a sound like, *yech*, and Margaret grimaces. Doris leans down, picks it up, and puts it back on my bun.

"I am *not* eating that," I inform her. "They're made from cow brains, you know."

Doris blinks at me through her thick lenses. "Actually, hot dogs are a blend of pork, beef, chicken, and turkey. *Not* cow brains." As if to prove her point, she takes a bite of her own and happily munches away. I should know better than to argue with Doris. She's in the gifted program for math and science. Oscar Mayer probably calls her to consult on the chemistry of their wieners.

I steal a potato chip from Alyssa's lunch, glancing around at my friends. They're all busy eating. No one has remembered. And to think I've been nervous all morning, waiting for this moment. Margaret and Doris are talking about their brainiac math teacher's new hairdo. Apparently, it's the square root of ugly. Lizzy and Alyssa are talking about track. Track? Since when are they interested in running around in circles? None of them seems to care that I promised to show them a script from my newest movie project today. I thought for sure someone would have asked about it by now. I guess it's lucky they've forgotten, since I don't have it anyway. I haven't written a single word. Still, the least they could do is seem . . . disappointed.

I chew on a fingernail, since I don't have anything else to eat. Finally, I can't stand it any longer. "So, I guess you guys probably want to know what kind of movie I decided to make."

They all stop talking and gaze at me. Alyssa pops a chip in her mouth. "Oh, yeah, what did you finally decide on?"

I take a deep, dramatic breath. "I'm *completely* stuck. I mean it. I need help."

"Make a zombie sequel," Lizzy says right away.

I finished making my first-ever full-length movie last semester, called *Night of the Zombie Chickens*. I've been telling my friends for weeks that I'm starting a new movie, but the truth is, I'm kind of nervous. I made *Night of the Zombie Chickens* for fun. I figured only my friends and family would see it. Then, my parents rented the old Roxy Theater downtown for a premiere, and the newspaper wrote a story about it. Lots of kids from school and even some teachers came to see it. Now, students come up to me in the hallway and beg to be in my next movie. Everyone wants to know what it's going to be about, which is probably why I have writer's block.

Alyssa makes a face. "No more zombies, please. I'm tired of getting splattered with blood."

"I know!" Margaret says. "Make a musical!"

My eyes bulge at the idea. For *Night of the Zombie Chickens*, I had to work with my mother's evil diva hens, who tried to ruin my life. That was bad enough. But directing a bunch of yowling middle schoolers?

"Sure," I say, always the diplomat. "That could work."

"I thought you were going to make a romance this time," Alyssa says loudly. "Remember?"

I never said the word *romance*. When Alyssa mentioned

it, I didn't say no, either. I guess that sounds like *yes* to a seventh grader who's eager to have a romantic scene with a certain somebody. Alyssa has a secret crush on Jake Knowles, except everyone has pretty much figured it out. Even Jake, probably. Alyssa is the only one who doesn't know that everyone knows. So, like I said, it's a secret.

Doris removes her glasses and polishes them with a greasy napkin. "You should make a movie about dark energy. Did you know that dark energy makes up seventy percent of the universe? You and me and everything on Earth—all the planets and stars everywhere—all the matter, we only make up five percent."

She holds her glasses up to the light. They look even more smeared than before. Margaret snatches them from her and takes a tiny spray bottle from her backpack. She mists the lenses and polishes them with a special cloth, then hands them back. Doris squints through her squeaky-clean glasses and blinks. She's probably never seen the world so clearly before. She peers at us to see if these mind-blowing facts are sinking in. "Isn't that cool?"

"Yeah. Wow." I try my best to look like my mind is blown.

Brave Margaret asks the question the rest of us are avoiding. "So, what *is* dark energy?"

Doris's eyes light up. "It's some kind of mysterious dark force. Einstein predicted that empty space wasn't really empty. That it has its own energy. Scientists think it's pulling the galaxies farther apart. But you can't see it and they can't prove it's really there."

Alyssa leans forward. "Then how would we make a movie about it?" The only dark energy she cares about involves a romantic scene with Jake Knowles.

"You could show a scientist trying to discover this huge mystery of the universe," Margaret offers. "She could sing a song about the stars," she adds dreamily.

Alyssa rolls her eyes. "That sounds thrilling."

"Well, it's more exciting than a romance," Margaret shoots back.

"Well, I vote for werewolves," Lizzy says.

My friends are not much help.

I'm about to jump in before they start arguing, when I see something fly past our heads from the corner of my eye. A moment later, Paul Corbett bellows at the next table. A slimy handful of green beans is sliding down his hair onto his collar.

Our heads snap around to see if Lunch Lady saw what happened. Luckily, she's yelling at some poor sixth grader on the other side of the room. Most of the lunch ladies at our school are moms who volunteer. They have names, like Mrs. Daley or Mrs. O'Neill. Lunch Lady is different. For one thing, no one knows her real name, which is why we have to call her Lunch Lady. There's a rumor she escaped from a loony bin and is hiding out at our school, waiting until the coast is clear. It might be true, because Lunch

Lady is always there and she's always watching us. Her hair is an odd rusty color, permed into little corkscrews, which she keeps flattened to her head with a black net. She has swinging folds of arm flesh and big hammy hands and fingers that remind me of miniature boiled hot dogs. No one misbehaves when Lunch Lady is nearby.

Paul whips his head around and shouts, "Who threw that?" He stares at everyone behind him, searching for a telltale smirk, a guilty face.

Even though we haven't done anything, it's important to *look* like we haven't done anything. Otherwise, Paul might decide to make our lives miserable. Luckily, we're old hands at this. Alyssa is lazily stirring her chocolate milk. Doris is eyeing my hot dog like she might stick it in her backpack for an afternoon snack. Lizzy doodles on a napkin. I'm gazing off into space, nibbling on a potato chip, the kung fu master of humble innocence. Paul's eyes practically scorch us with their glare, but there are a lot of kids sitting behind him and they probably all have their reasons for throwing something at him.

I hate food fights, ever since a chewed-up piece of ketchup-covered hot dog once hit me in the face. Still, if anyone deserves wet, slimy green beans in his hair, it's Paul Corbett. Lizzy has her back to Paul, so she's making funny faces at us, mimicking him. Margaret can't help it; a tiny smile escapes. Big mistake.

Paul's eyes narrow. "What are you laughing at, Margerine? You think it's funny? Did you throw those?"

Paul and Blake Nash pick on a lot of kids, but they keep their worst for Margaret. She's an easy target because she's so nice. Sad to say, but nice can be hazardous to your health in middle school. Plus, she has red hair, freckles, and crooked teeth. She used to be completely ignored until last semester, when she got the lead part in the musical *Annie*. Since then, people have been a little nicer to Margaret, except for Paul. If anything, he's been worse. He points a finger at Margaret. "You're dead, Red." He grabs the beans out of his hair and throws them on the floor.

"Just what do you think you're doing?" a voice bellows. We all freeze. Lunch Lady steams up the aisle, arm flesh flapping, pointing at the beans. "Pick those up right now!" Her mammoth chest heaves with indignation as she glares down at Paul. I'm pretty sure Lunch Lady would protect that lunchroom floor with her last, dying breath.

"Someone threw them at me," Paul whines.

Lunch Lady's face scrunches up even tighter. She's like a teakettle on boil, right before it shoots out steam and starts screaming. Paul jumps up fast and starts picking up beans. Every kid at our table is grinning. It's like the time a guy in a convertible Porsche roared past my dad and me on the highway, probably going a hundred miles an hour. My dad looked mad, but also a little jealous, and grumbled something about rotten drivers. When we saw the Porsche pulled over by a highway patrol car a few miles later, my dad smacked his hands together and waved, grinning, as we drove past. He hummed under his breath for the next fifty miles. It pretty much made his day.

That's how we all feel about Paul getting down on the floor, picking up slimy beans. Finally, justice is served.

The bell rings and we move to dump our garbage. Suddenly, Margaret nudges me. "Look, there's the new boy. His family moved here from New York City."

We all turn and watch as a boy stacks his tray. You can tell right away he's not local. There's something about his clothes and his haircut and his look. I can't figure out exactly what it is. It's just a striped shirt. And it's just some dark blond hair falling into one eye. He's not real tall or big. But somehow, put it all together, and it's one step beyond cool. It's cool without trying to look cool.

I'm so busy staring, I almost miss the garbage can as I toss my spare body part hot dog. "Wow," I murmur.

"Wow," Lizzy agrees.

Doris also gazes at him through her thick glasses. "I just remembered something. I heard he's like you, Kate."

"Wha-at?" I say, stunned. "He likes me?"

I haven't even met the kid! Could he possibly have seen me in the hallway and developed one of those instant crushes? A tiny, secret part of me is thrilled. A cool boy from NYC likes *me*? My mind starts fast-pedaling into the future, imagining our first meeting, shy smiles, my witty remarks, his glowing admiration. In another minute, we'll be married with kids if I don't slow down.

"No, I said he's *like* you," Doris repeats. "I mean, he also likes to make movies, like you."

"Oh. Yeah, I thought that sounded weird." I try to sound nonchalant. Still, it's embarrassing. Lizzy and Alyssa are grinning at each other. My head, which expanded like a hot air balloon, now shrinks smaller than a week-old wiener. Of course he doesn't like me. Why would he? I'm just a boring kid with braces and frizzy brown hair. No boy is ever going to like me, especially with Alyssa standing right next to me. I sigh as I look at her. Tall, perfect teeth, shiny blond hair. She may not understand the scientific theory of dark energy but I'm pretty sure that isn't what seventh-grade boys care about.

I'm just lucky no one heard me except my friends. Someone like Paul Corbett or Tina Turlick might have run over to the new boy and started screaming things like, *Kate Walden thinks you like her! She thinks you have a big crush on her!* Middle school is like that—a series of social land mines just waiting to explode in your face. Even though I know it's unfair, I feel a tiny stab of resentment toward the new boy. What is he, too good for me? I'm not sure which surprises me more, that this kid likes to make movies or that Doris heard and passed along a piece of gossip.

"Really, he makes movies? You actually heard that?"

Doris adjusts her glasses. "Noah Fleming told me in Biology."

Noah Fleming is like Doris reincarnated as a boy. He's a supersmart science geek. He's not bad looking, in a tall, skinny way, but his nerd factor totally outweighs his cute factor. Plus, Paul and Blake stuck him with the unfortunate nickname Nose Phlegmy.

I peer at Doris. "How did Noah hear that?"

"Noah's locker is near Tristan's, so they were talking. I guess Noah mentioned you and your movie. That's his name—Tristan Kingsley."

Tristan. Jeez, even his name is cool. A strange tingling starts in my face. People were talking about me. The new boy from NYC was talking about *me*. He probably did a double take when he heard I've already made a feature-length movie. It *is* just a little impressive. The tingle turns to a warm glow. And then it hits me. Noah's locker is just down from mine. That means Tristan's locker is near mine, too. We can talk movies together. It will be so great to have a filmmaker buddy! A cool NYC filmmaker buddy with blond hair falling in one eye.

2

I'm still pondering my movie as I head for the bus after school. It's early April and most of the snow has melted into gray slush. I hate my clunky snow boots so I left them at home. Now, the cold slop seeps into my sneakers. By the time I climb on the bus, my feet are soaked. I slide in next to Lizzy and she grins and removes her earbuds.

Lizzy Chang's family moved to Medford when she was in fifth grade. Her parents speak with an accent and Lizzy speaks perfect English and perfect Chinese. Sometimes, just for fun, or when she's mad, she'll talk to herself in Chinese so we don't know what she's saying. We're all good friends but Mimi Reynolds is her BFF. Mimi's family moved to Texas a month ago, so it's been a tough time for Lizzy. She's tiny, even shorter than me. Some people make a mistake and think she's delicate, like a china doll. Really, Lizzy's more like the Great Wall of China. Have a run-in with her and she'll be the last one standing. She's tough and funny and, best of all, she likes making movies.

Olivia Sykes leans forward from the seat behind us. "Anything exciting happen in school today?"

"Why weren't you in gym class?" Lizzy asks.

Olivia pops her gum. "A field trip. We went to the art museum."

"No fair!" Lizzy exclaims. "Why didn't we get to go?"

Olivia shrugs. "It was fun."

Lizzy loves painting and crafty stuff. She can take fabric and whip up a cute toy or purse while the rest of us are still staring at our material, trying to figure out what to do.

Olivia lowers her voice. "Jack Timner got in trouble at the museum today."

Lizzy grins. "What'd he do?"

We both glance toward the back of the bus where Jack sits. He isn't a bad kid, but he can't settle down. He's always trying to be the center of attention. He'll do any stupid thing if he thinks someone will laugh, which lands him in trouble a lot. Jack isn't laughing now, though. His face is sullen, legs splayed out in the aisle. He's probably hoping someone will trip over them.

Jack suddenly looks up and catches my eye, like he knows we're talking about him. He glares and I look away. Both his parents are ex-military. I heard they crack down hard on Jack and have threatened to send him to military school. No wonder he looks glum.

"He pretended like he was going to draw on a painting," Olivia whispers.

I give a delighted gasp of horror. Even I know that is serious. That's like joking on an airplane that you hope the bomb in your suitcase doesn't go off. "Are you kidding? What happened?"

"He was holding up a marker near a painting, trying to be funny for his buddies, and two guards ran over shouting at him. They grabbed him and took him away, and Mr. Graves had to go talk to the museum director. Now Jack can't go on any more field trips and he's got about a month of detentions. They called his parents." Olivia makes a face. "You know what that means."

I risk another glance at Jack. That's when I notice Tristan Kingsley sitting in the seat behind Jack. I quickly turn around. I can hardly believe my luck. The cute moviemaking boy from New York City rides my bus.

Olivia taps me on the shoulder. "So when do you start your next movie? I really want to be a zombie."

"Haven't you heard?" Lizzy says importantly. "No zombies this time. Kate's going to do something completely different. She's just not sure what."

"Oh, I know!" Olivia squeals. "You *HAVE* to do a vampire movie! Vampires would be SO cool. And we could make it really scary. Everyone would want to be in it!"

I try not to roll my eyes. Vampires are so overdone.

"I keep telling her it should have werewolves," Lizzy says. "Werewolves are cool."

"They are," Olivia admits, "but they're too furry. Who wants to look like a rabid dog? Vampires are hot."

The bus chugs up to Lizzy and Olivia's stop. They're still debating werewolves versus vampires as they get off. It's Jack Timner's stop, too. His backpack hits me in the back of the head as he goes by. Probably payback for staring at him. "Sorry," he calls over his shoulder, smirking.

Hot vampires, hairy werewolves—I sigh and lean back. I'm pretty sure Alyssa doesn't want to wear fangs or fur. It's great that so many kids want to be in my movie, but I'm going to need someone to help me control the chaos. I need an assistant. Who would be right for the job? I stare out the window at the bare trees flying past. Gray slush splatters the dirty snow mounded on the curbs as we pass by. Winter always drags on too long, like one of those boring black-and-white foreign films that never ends. I slip off my shoes. My socks are wet and my toes feel like tiny blocks of ice.

The bus slows down as we enter a development on the edge of town. It's called Deer Hollow even though the deer are long gone. This area used to be full of trees but now it's lined with big, fancy houses. We stop at a new home and Tristan swings past and hurries down the bus steps. I watch him walk up the long driveway. What kind of movies has he made? Most likely short ones with his friends. He would

probably love to help make a ~~...~~ movie. That's when it
hits me. Tristan would be the pe~~r~~ assistant director! I
may not be a big-time Hollywood play~~...~~ but I can teach
him what I've learned so far.

We stop at a few more houses in Deer Ho~~...~~ I'm
the last person on the bus. Sal, the bus driver, h~~...~~
another ten minutes on country roads to reach my ~~...~~
I sigh and wish for the millionth time that my family ~~...~~
moved to Deer Hollow instead of a run-down farmhouse
in the middle of nowhere. The funny thing is, we have tons
of deer. All the ones that got chased off by the mega-house
invasion must have headed over to our place.

Sal glances at me through the big mirror over his head.
I always feel bad for him because he has a girl's name. He's
Italian and I guess it's short for Salvatore. The boys on the
bus all call him Sally but he doesn't seem to mind.

"You decided what your next movie's about, Kate?" he
calls out. Sal's a big film buff. He even came to my premiere.

"I'm not sure. Maybe a romance."

Sal twists his lower lip, like he sucked on a lemon.
"Romance? Hmmm. Could be tricky."

"Yeah, I know."

The bus finally wheezes to a stop outside our house and
I hurry up the aisle. "Crime drama," Sal says out of the
corner of his mouth, like he's offering me a shady tip on
a horse race. "Italian mafia. Hasn't been done well since
The Godfather." He taps his head. "I got all kinds of stories.

From my grandfather, abo... ...ne old days. Somebody needs
to make it into a movi... ...tracks. "Your grandfather was in
This stops me...
the mafia?" ...this is a funny joke. "No, no, no. Maybe."
Sal la... ...e knew people who knew people."
He s... ...g to ask Sal if he's in the mafia too, but if he
...it, then he might have to kill me so I couldn't tell
...e.

"I'll think about it," I promise.

What I'm really thinking about as I swing off the bus is
how great it would be to have a cute A.D. from NYC helping me on my next project. The thought warms my insides,
all the way down to my frozen feet.